PROBO'S LAMENT

The *True* Adventures of a Small-town Elephant
in the City of Big Shoulders

To Richard EBY —
Forty-five years
and this is all I
could come up with?
well, I hope it
brings you a few
laughs ANYWAY.
— Gene 4/2011

Gene Lubin

Illustrated by
Howard Berkman

New American Storybook

New American Storybook
P.O. Box 597920
Chicago, Illinois 60659

www.newamericanstorybook.com

This is a work of fiction. Any references to historical events, real or previously existing organizations, real people, or real locales are used fictitiously. Other names, characters, places, incidents, and groups are the product of the author's imagination, and any resemblance to actual events, locales or persons, living or dead, is entirely coincidental.

Warning: This book is not intended for children. It contains material of a suggestive or adult nature which may be unsuitable for younger or more sensitive readers.

Third Printing, Revised

ISBN 978-0-9822559-0-2

1. Satire. 2. Comic adventure.

PRINTED IN THE UNITED STATES OF AMERICA

CONTENTS

"Fear not," said the enchantress. "You will find your way home, and before you do you will discover that we're all in this together...you, me, Opie, even the twins. Like you, we live in a world where everything of any real value has been trivialized beyond recognition – even language itself. The fact is, the rabbit-hole down which we've been led is made up of *words*, not images. Sometimes the only way to deal with all this absurdity is to counter it with some absurdities of your own, and by so doing once again become master of your own voice. The truth is, Probo, if you don't live by your own illusions you'll live by somebody else's. That is the only reality."

PROBO'S LAMENT

The ~True~ Adventures of a Small-town Elephant
in the City of Big Shoulders

NOTICE

Be it ordained by the common Council of the city of Fort Wayne, That every person and all persons desiring to exhibit any menagerie, caravan, animal or collection of animals, circus, theater, or theatrical or comical performance, or any natural curiosity, wax works, or figures, or any feats of tumbling, slight of hand, rope or wire dancing, necromancy or ventriloquism, within the limits of said city, shall first obtain from the Mayor and city Clerk of said city a license permitting such exhibition...The rate to be charged by the Mayor for any such license, shall not be less than five or more than fifty dollars.

As posted in the
August 27, 1857 edition of
The Fort Wayne Weekly Times
Fort Wayne, Indiana

Beware the Evil Bastard with the Big Rubber Nose

1. Circus Days

Shakey, with the wooden leg, could really blow that thing. You could almost hear a pin drop when he raised his long, sleek proboscis high into the air and let go with a soaring obbligato that sent the Fat Lady into throes of ecstasy and brought the hometown audience and visiting rubes to their feet. Mumps the orangutan was visibly jealous, as was his good pal, Probo - though the talented elephant lad had little cause to feel that way given that when he cut loose on that horn of his the young cows out behind the barn went crazy, kicking over their buckets and sending their trainers into fits of frenzy. Nevertheless, it was the one-legged anteater that everyone came to see. As the closing strains of *God Bless America* resonated throughout the big top the clarinet player would hobble up to the front of the stage dragging his heavy, wooden appendage behind him and sporting a well-rehearsed look of anguish on his impeccably groomed snout. This prompted an even greater response from the ecstatic onlookers, while the indignant trumpet player and his brooding companion waited on the sidelines hoping the ringmaster in his fancy, red jacket might yet acknowledge their presence to the departing crowd.

One afternoon as rehearsal was coming to an end Mumps looked up from his instrument and whispered to the elephant,

"I've had it with Peanutville. I'm ready to hit the road and head out for the city. Wanna join me?" Probo had heard this kind of talk before. The ape was always threatening to pull up stakes and leave the circus, complaining about how a first-class primate such as himself shouldn't have to play second fiddle to some miserable 'bug-eater'. It galled him, too, to see so many of his not-so-distant relatives filing into the big top on Sunday afternoons in their mail-order monkey suits and OshKosh B'Goshs just to see some paraplegic who whistled through his nose.

"He's not a paraplegic," Probo would admonish his petulant friend, but the ape would simply frown and say, "He's no musician either, in my book." Mumps had illusions of playing in a fancy club somewhere with one of those south-of-the-border bands and a couple of Latino beauties shaking their big, hand-painted maracas and balancing fresh bunches of bananas atop their fruit-laden heads. Probo, who wasn't quite the dreamer his friend was, tried to convince the starry-eyed orangutan that groups like that probably didn't have much need for a bow-legged bassoon player who leaps from trees. Besides, he added, most musicians would consider themselves lucky to perform alongside a renowned woodwind player of the stature of Shakey. Perhaps it was this well intentioned but ill-stated advice that further inflamed the ape's animosity toward the anteater, while Probo for the most part kept his own feelings to himself. It was bad enough, he figured, that he'd been compelled to speak out concerning the glaring omission to the colorful, new circus posters plastered all over town. Here it was, well into July - and still, his was the only name missing from the ubiquitous show bills announcing the start of the '84 season and listing the various performers to be featured that year.

Probo took his complaint to the great man himself, Cecil B. DeMoyel, but the old circus master wasn't as sharp as he used to be. He simply nodded and said he would look into the matter…and that was the end of that.

What Probo and the orangutan failed to take into account were the anteater's many acts of kindness toward them. Did he not call in sick on several occasions just to give the bassoon player a chance at the spotlight? And did he not once save the young pygmy elephant with his horn wailing blindly in the air from stumbling off the bandstand into a pile of horse waste - no doubt left there by Harry the Happy Gelding during one of his more spiteful moods? Fact is, Shakey wasn't all that bad a guy. He had earned his nickname long before the terrible accident that took his leg, due in part to his habit of trembling like some sugar junkie all hopped up on blue cotton candy each time he broke into one of his frenetic clarinet solos. "That boy's on *something*," his fans would say laughingly, winking at one another. Others claimed he played even better *after* the accident - the convulsive tremors of his savage vibrato traveling down through his prosthetic limb into the floor of the old bandstand, thereby creating an inaudible rumble that set the trick dogs to howling and their scantily-clad trainers to squirming in place. Probo knew, of course, that it was the soaring glissando of his own incomparable horn playing that put the ants in the beautiful showgirls' pants…and not the antics of the pretentious anteater with his one-legged Elvis impersonations.

Despite their differences, these three soulful companions made some beautiful music together. It would be a shame for them

The three soulful companions made some beautiful music together.

to split up over such petty differences. Probo sat mulling this over one afternoon while wolfing down a snout-full of 'salted ones' and drawing long, cool drafts from a nearby bucket. Sometimes, at moments like this he would feel pangs of remorse over the many occasions on which, in an effort to cheer up the downcast ape, he'd made some offhand remark...something like, "Yea, you the *Man*, monkey," or "You pass gas better than that bug-eater blows scales." Probo was beginning to realize that by playing on the ape's sensibilities he was simply avoiding having to face up to his own hostility toward the anteater. Elephants may be users, but they're capable of being painfully honest at times.

While contemplating thus, Probo sifted through piles of discarded shells hoping to find a Spanish beauty or two he might have overlooked. His failing eyesight was still bothering him, and he was debating whether to follow the lead of some of the other elephants and a few of the shaggy-haired humans who had been experimenting lately with the curious, new medicine that had been going around. Suddenly, who should appear but 'the Man' himself, looking dark and sullen as usual. "Peanuts again, eh?" he grumbled, kicking at the ground.

"Hey, what's up, Swinger?" Probo sang out in yet another misguided attempt to lift the lumbering ape's spirits. Time was when everyone called him Swinger, not because of his skills as a musician, or the way he would swing from the tent masts on opening nights throwing half-eaten fruits and other unmentionables down on the spectators - but because of his reputation as a man about town. There wasn't a simian this side of Sumatra who didn't want to dip into the handsome orangutan's gene pool. Then, one day a bad case of the mumps laid him low. When they told him afterwards he would never be able to father children, he lost all confidence in himself, both on stage and off…so to speak. He would turn tail and run any time a couple of auburn beauties would saunter up to him and ask, "Hey there big boy…got any extra bananas?" One more reason the proud but disheartened ape hated the clarinet player with the bushy tail and long, sinuous tongue. It seems the latter had himself earned something of a reputation of late for his prowess with the ladies.

While Probo had some compassion for his large but impotent monkey friend, he had little or none for the anteater. After all, it was the bug-eater's own fault, sniffing around the bear cage where he had no business being. When the bear finally shit out the leg five days later, someone was heard to say that it looked "as white and shiny as an elephant's tusk." Probo, like all young bulls, being self-conscious and a bit unsure of himself, immediately assumed that the bristly South American with the severed limb had heard about the remark and thereafter harbored a secret resentment toward him and elephants in general. Everyone assured the high-strung trumpet player that his fears were unfounded…but Probo's paranoid tendencies did not go unnoticed.

Well, emotions are a complicated business. In the end it was the doubt-ridden pachyderm, not the disgruntled ape that slipped off one evening under cover of darkness and headed for the highway. It had all been too much for him…the nagging suspicions…the feelings of guilt…the sleepless hours listening to the anteater in the stall next to him sucking up to the young beavers and other woodland animals that sneaked under the canopy at night to pay homage to their hero. Then, too, there was that evil bastard with the stupid bicycle horn and big, rubber nose who was always whispering in his ear - suggesting that perhaps it was the *anteater* that was responsible for the elephant's name being left off the shiny, new circus posters. But then, everyone knew the obnoxious funnyman had his own agenda. Hadn't he been heard practicing in the wee hours of the morning when everyone was asleep? Not that the clown's skills with the coronet were any match for his more accomplished rival; but there was talk that the gawky, six-foot-something giant had hopes of someday giving up the greasepaint and taking the trumpet player's place on the Peanutville stage.

Yes, it was all a bit too much for Probo. He was a Libra, and Libras hate conflict. Moreover, he had Pisces rising, with the moon in Leo and Pluto in the seventh house - also known as *'House Harkonen'* according to Madam Zuzu, the fortune teller. But then, the crazy old woman had been snorting a bit too much of the *Spice* anyway - ever since reading Frank Herbert's science fiction classic <u>DUNE.</u>

2. On the Road

It was late January when Probo packed up his meager belongings and slipped out the back gate leading to the highway. Most of the animals were hunkered down for the winter, the circus grounds deserted, the out-buildings shuttered and tucked away like Christmas cottages in a Currier and Ives print. No one would notice he was missing, except possibly the old groundskeeper with the fuzzy whiskers and jolly, red cheeks who came around checking on things; but he seemed to be pretty much out of it anyway, spending most of his time soaking up the holiday spirits with Madam Zuzu and that evil bastard, Hornbuckle, behind closed doors. Probo was relieved that he would no longer have to endure the malicious laughter and other ungodly sounds emanating from that broken-down trailer of theirs.

In the months that followed, Probo traveled from town to town putting long miles between himself and the glamorous world of high-flying acrobats and prancing ponies he'd been born and raised in. Here and there he performed odd jobs for the local farmers, hauling firewood or pulling stalled vehicles from the snow…anything that would earn him a bite to eat and a place to spend the night. As winter turned to spring he landed a position with a small children's zoo a few hours outside of Chicago. It was comprised mainly of sheep and goats with a few ducks and chickens thrown in and some games of chance for the adults. Probo originally had been hired to play his trumpet and welcome visitors to the roadside menagerie, but he soon found himself playing host to a bunch of snot-nosed eleven-year-olds who took greater delight in snuffing their cigarettes out in his back than posing for photographs with the sad-faced pachydem or stroking his trunk. Fortunately, elephants have tough hides - so Probo accepted his plight, hoping to move on to something better at the earliest opportunity.

One brisk morning who should Probo run into, but his old pal, Opie. The skinny, freckle-faced youth with the shock of straw-colored hair had been a member of the Peanutville band up until about six months prior to Probo's departure, at which time he announced that he was heading off in search of fame and fortune. Since then the only fortune the lanky drummer had amassed was the few dollars he earned playing with small pick-up bands he met along the road. At present he was on his way home to visit his grandmother who lived in a small town in Wisconsin called Mada-pa-hada-wanee…a name taken from an old Indian expression dating back to the 1700s when some of the local tribes were fighting the French. It meant 'kill the pantywaist bastards and take their women.' When the British moved in they decided they liked the name, and kept it. According to Opie there was another town about six miles down the road, called Hada-pa-wada-manee, which meant 'I slept with one of the pantywaist bastards…and I liked it!'

Opie was a decent bloke, not the sharpest knife in the

drawer, but not someone you wouldn't have a drink with now and then. And that's exactly what they did. The former bandmates parked themselves in front of the beer and brats stand and began talking about old times, their recent travels, their problems with women (problem was, neither of them had any)…and just about anything, so long as it didn't touch upon the forbidden subject of why the elephant had run off from the circus. *That* at least, the talkative Wisconsin kid had the good sense not to mention. He simply played dumb (which took no great effort) and congratulated his glum-looking companion on having given up the dreary life of a circus performer for a glamorous career bringing joy and laughter to prepubescent corn-huskers who'd learned to chew and spit tobacco before they could walk. "At least you got top billing…just as you always wanted," piped the drummer, nodding toward the makeshift sign stuck along the roadside announcing the addition of a 'REAL LIVE ELAPHENT' to the zoo.

As the beer flowed and the conversation rambled Opie began to open up about his childhood, something he had been reticent about in the past. He explained how he had been raised by his grandmother, an old-time carny who went by the name of Betty 'Bumps' due to the many years she'd spent operating the bumper cars and other attractions at carnivals and amusement parks throughout the Midwest. She had taken Opie in after his father, an auctioneer with an incurable stutter, turned to drink and his mother ran off with an antiques dealer she'd met at an estate sale while her unsuspecting husband was hung up on his '*T*'s. Apparently he'd been calling out some items for bid when he came across a rare, 1922 Tommy Tittlemouse truck and tractor set…made in Tortuga. By the time the man with the unfortunate speech impediment had finished with little Tommy and was just getting his mouth wrapped around the insurmountable *'Tit'...*, the antiques dealer had dragged his wife out behind the barn and was hauling ass.

At first, Betty's restless young charge found life living out of his grandmother's trailer not all that appealing. He often thought of his parents and dreamt of the day when he would become the great communicator his father had only hoped to be...someone who could talk like a politician and separate the suckers from their money like a Las Vegas whore. An attorney, perhaps. But when the lad discovered how much could be made working the carnival circuit, he gave up any notions of standing before the bench, and went in instead for hustling clems along the midway.

Anyway, this grandmother of Opie's was quite a gal. Besides spinning toddlers around all day on the carnival rides, she had this little S&M thing going after hours while the rest of the crew were asleep or in town getting drunk. Rumor was, she would round up some of the local thrill-seeking farm boys, fill them full of moonshine and lure them onto the carousel where she would whip their naked butts with a riding crop as they whirled around to the winsome sounds of the calliope. Some say she even went so far as to gather up some old farm implements and latch them onto the back of the merry-go-round horses just to make those high-flying plowboys feel at home. One night, while the curious seven-year-old was supposed to be asleep, the local sheriff came around making inquiries. The boy's grandmother went to the door of their little trailer and presented herself as a quiet homemaker who stayed up late baking cookies. The sheriff, having a bit of a sweet tooth himself, dropped the matter precipitously once the woman invited him in for a glass of schnapps and a generous helping of sweet potato pie. "I never touch that sweet potato pie no more," said the drummer to his elephant friend, a strange look wafting across his face.

As the alcohol did its work, further loosening the Wisconsin lad's tongue, the discussion shifted from stories about his childhood to rumors he'd heard recently concerning the one-legged anteater and the bassoon-playing ape...how they had settled their differences and become best of friends, working out woodwind arrangements that were knocking their socks off back in Peanutville. Not only that, but they had recruited the clown as Probo's replacement for the new circus season which was currently underway. With perseverance and long hours of practice they had turned the funnyman into a fairly respectable musician, at least insofar as the leaden ears of the circus audiences could discern. Well, maybe the young cows out behind the barn weren't all that impressed, but the old cows were...and that was good enough for the lecherous clown and the long-suffering ape.

"That son of a bitch!" cried Probo as the news of his betrayal sank in. "It was that red-haired banana sucker all along! I should have known. And that evil bastard, Hornbuckle...I thought there was something fishy about the way he was always acting real nice to me and inquiring about my health. Everyone knows clowns aren't really friendly. What's friendly about someone who *paints* a smile on?"

The enraged elephant began stomping at the ground, waving his trunk about and making shrill trumpeting sounds that sent a handful of customers and a flurry of ducks scrambling for cover. It looked as if any moment he might stampede right through the refreshment stand, sending popcorn and cheese-dogs flying in all directions. Then, all at once he stopped, swung around in the drummer's direction and stared at his ruddy-faced companion with a fearsome expression. "Oh, oh," thought the Wisconsin lad. "I'd better get out of here. He looks madder than a pit bull with one of those Dober-men up its ass." You could always tell when someone was from Madapahadawanee - especially a gumball like Opie.

Glancing at his watch and mumbling something about the time and how his grandmother was waiting for him, Opie began staggering toward his red pick-up truck a short distance away. Before he got very far, however, he felt the elephant's long, powerful trunk wrap itself around his narrow waist like a boa constrictor trying to squeeze the breath out of a lamppost. "Hold on there, Little Red Riding Hood," said Probo, tightening his grip on the frightened youth. "I see you're still driving that old beater of yours. I've been thinking about heading up to Chicago to see if I can land a job with a decent band there. You wouldn't mind if I rode along with you a ways, would you - seeing as you'll be going in that direction anyhow?" The anxious drummer took no time in responding. "Sure, no problem...no problem at all," he cried as the boa constrictor released its grip allowing the dim light at the top of the lamppost to flicker back on. "Glad to have you along. Er...you're not still mad, are you?"

"Home is where the horn is," Probo sighed,
climbing into the back of Opie's truck.

"Mad? Who's mad? I'm just a little…perturbed," said the pachyderm, looking somewhat embarrassed. "What do I care what they do back in Peanutville? I'm on my way to better things. Come on, I'll help you move the drums and stuff around in the back of your truck. A little wind in my face might do me some good."

Opie breathed a sigh of relief as he pulled the keys from his pocket and once again headed toward the parking lot. "By the way…," he called out, glancing over his shoulder. "All that, er, extra weight might put a bit of a strain on the gas tank…if you know what I mean." Probo bit his lip in an effort to restrain his temper. "Yea, sure…I know what you mean. But all those beers I paid for don't seem to have put much of a strain on that hollow leg of yours. I remember those nights back in Peanutville when you'd kill off a six-pack, lay a brick up against the gas pedal and go tearing down the highway with your ass hanging out the window, mooning at every car you'd pass. Well, I'll tell you what…get me to Chicago in one piece, and I'll give you some money for gas once we arrive. I'm not handing it to you now so you can ditch me at the first rest stop we come to. I'm not that stupid. Right now, I need to collect my belongings and talk to the guy who runs this place. He owes me a week's pay."

"Won't he be pissed if you just up and quit without giving him a week's notice?" asked the drummer, hoping to wrangle himself free of his obligation. Probo threw the goofy-looking kid a reproachful look. "Listen man…if that bozo had a clue about anything, he'd be cozying up to that sweet, young thing behind the cashier's cage instead of petting sheep all day."

23

Probo's Lament

And so it was that Probo made his way to the big city, intent on leaving bitter memories behind him and starting a new life. Not an unusual beginning for a young man on the make. Lots of aspiring artists had left home to seek their fortune. Many returned rich and famous. Difference was, he might never be going back. "Ah well, home is where the horn is," sighed Probo, fitting his trumpet into the cheap cardboard suitcase he always carried and settling himself into the back of Opie's '64 Chevy with the faded circus logo on the side. He had no idea what to expect from a city not known to have a fondness for elephants. Chicago was a Democrat's town. Anyone even remotely resembling a Republican was shot on sight.

3. A Perfectly Matched Set of Choppers

The day had turned warm and breezy by the time the two circus buddies reached the shores of Lake Michigan - not unusual for the first week in May, but more than had been expected after a chilly morn. They had barely made it as far as they did, what with Opie's truck coughing and wheezing like some Paleolithic beast in the throes of death. As they pulled into a gas station a short distance from the sprawling lakefront, the creature threw a rod and gave up the ghost with a violent shudder. "Now what?" Opie cried excitedly. "How am I going to get home? And what about my drums? How's about it, Probo? What about that money you promised me?"

"Money? What money, man? I already gave you the ten dollars we agreed upon so you could pig out on chili dogs and chocolate covered raisins during that stop we made back in Peoria. I haven't got a cent to spare." Opie glared at the grim-faced elephant in disbelief. "But you just got paid," he argued. "You told me so yourself. Surely, you can lend me a little extra so I can buy a bus ticket home to Wisconsin. I'll mail it back to you as soon as I get there. Just give me your address..."

"My address? Do I look like I have a suite at the Ritz

waiting for me? Come on, man…think of *my* situation. I have to feed myself and find a place to stay while I look for a job. I've barely got enough to get by. Wait a minute…I have an idea! I saw a currency exchange a few blocks back as we were driving in. Maybe you can phone your grandmother and have her wire you some money. Or perhaps you can pick up a few bucks selling what's left of your buggy here for scrap."

"Sell her for scrap! Are you crazy?" exclaimed the heartbroken drummer, tears pouring from his eyes. "You might as well tell someone to sell their dead mother's body to a medical school so they can buy a new set of tires."

"Yea? Well, if it included a free car wash, you'd probably go for it," Probo snapped angrily, stepping aside to admit a tall, burly man who was pushing his way between the pair with a menacing look. "Whoa…hold on there," said the gas station attendant, glancing at Opie's out of town plates. "You're in Chicago now, boys. You want somebody to take this baby off your hands, you'll have to pay *them*. But I'll tell you what…if you're interested I know a fellow out in Libertyville who collects old vehicles and parks them in his yard. Has a lot of fun propping dummies and whatnot up behind the wheel at Halloween to amuse the kids."

"Dummies, huh?" Opie said pensively, running his hand lovingly over the dead beast's fender. "Well, I suppose that'll work." Throwing his traveling companion a heartfelt glance, the drummer implored, "If I run over to that currency exchange for a while, will you be here when I get back?"

"Yea, sure," the elephant agreed reluctantly as the anxious twenty-year-old shuffled off down the street. In the meantime, a short tour of the area might be in order, Probo decided, heading off cheerfully in the opposite direction. Not far from the sparkling shore of Lake Michigan with its cozy, little harbor and sandy beaches stood glistening towers of glass and steel sandwiched in between older structures of mortar and brick. Each of these monuments to wealth and power had its own private driveway with a solicitous, well-heeled doorman to greet the residents as they returned home from a hard day of shopping at Gucci's or selling-off American interests to foreign investors down at the bank. A few blocks west of this pristine real estate, however, the scene changed dramatically. The streets grew dark and narrow, filled with abandoned walk-ups, run-down tenements and empty store fronts that had not seen a nail or a coat of paint in fifty years. Here and there were old mansions in various states of disrepair, many of which served as halfway houses for former addicts, recovering alcoholics and convicts out on parole. Others overflowed with people newly released from the nearby mental facilities as part of a cost-saving initiative heralded by the state's budget-minded governor as 'a great humanitarian effort'.

In the distance a string of nursing homes lined the thoroughfare, their lifeless inhabitants staring blankly through unwashed windows at a huge, ornate structure rising up in the middle of the block. The *Venetian Ballroom* was an old barn where many of these same, sad denizens of the boulevard had danced the night away back in their youth. Most of the great bands of the era had played there, including a group of local musicians who billed themselves as 'Daddy G and his Mellow Men'. This motley assortment of part-time soda jerks and weekend bell-hops boasted a fairly good horn section and a lead singer with a penchant for leading young women astray. The group managed to hang on into the psychedelic sixties, at which point they traded in their instruments for guitars and updated their repertoire in an effort to keep pace with the times. They grew their hair long (what they had left of it) and changed the band's name to Daddy G and his *Very* Mellow Men - which did little to impress the younger crowd, most of whom were too stoned to give a fig what these guys were about anyway. The group's final appearance at the Venetian Ballroom was a 1971 reunion of couples from the nearby retirement centers who came out to enjoy one last Fox Trot beneath the cavernous hall's star-studded canopy and the painted cupids smiling down from above. Daddy G, who was no spring chicken himself, ascended the bandstand slowly, removed something from his mouth which he deposited on the table behind him - then led the band in a raucous, hip-swirling rendition of *Let's Spend the Night Together*. As a half dozen or so hesitant couples ventured onto the dance floor, the aged singer spotted several women in the crowd with whom he had enjoyed an occasional indiscretion many years before. Of course, they had been a good deal younger then, as had he. Now, these prim and proper ladies with their hair tied up in neat, grey buns shuffled about with their doddering husbands at their sides. In what can only be described as an act of hubris, the vain and arrogant singer began calling out to them, shouting their names and making uninvited remarks such as, "Hey there Dorothy (or Mildred or Alice, etc.)...do you remember that night out behind the men's room before we went over to my place and got drunk as skunks?" As a result several ladies, humiliated beyond belief, passed out on the dance floor and had to be revived. Someone called for a glass of water, but all that could be had at the moment was one containing a perfectly matched set of yellowing choppers which smiled back at the defenseless women with an insatiable grin.

A few blocks north of the ballroom lay the old business district, once a bustling center for nightlife, drawing visitors from all over the city to its clubs, theaters, restaurants and the like. Little remained now, Probo observed, but the hulking shells of some boarded-up movie houses, a run-down diner or two and a seedy-looking bar. "So this is the City of the Big Shoulders," thought Probo, recalling a line from a Carl Sandburg poem his mother had read to him. "I wonder what else is big about it," he reflected, assuming the area he was in to be the armpit while the more unmentionable parts were somewhere to the south…in the vicinity of City Hall perhaps. "It sure doesn't look like the kind of place to find a job," he told himself. "Maybe I'd better chill out till morning and then move on."

Back at the gas station Probo stared at his watch and waited impatiently for Opie to return. The scrappy blond kid finally appeared, bounding up the sidewalk with a huge grin on his face. Apparently he had succeeded in getting in touch with his family and arranging for them to send him some money. That having been settled Probo could turn his attention to finding a room for the night, while Opie would continue on to his grandmother's house where he no doubt would find a nice piece of sweet potato pie waiting for him. "So what's the deal?" asked the elephant as the skinny Wisconsin kid caught his breath.

"Everything's great!" exclaimed the drummer. "The minute I told my grandma about our situation and where we are, she let out a loud whoop and said, *'Just stay put, boy. I feel like coming and cussing today.'*" Probo stared incredulously at the pimple-faced lad, wondering if he'd been chewing on some of that loco weed again or was just plain nuts. He then asked hesitantly, "Yes, and that means…?"

"That means she's on her way here. They should be arriving in a few hours, depending on the traffic. I told her we'd arrange with the gas station attendant to let them know where we are while we find a place to eat." Probo's face grew long. "Coming here?" he queried, his mind reeling with a thousand suspicions. "Why here…and who is *they*?"

"*They* would be the Gornisht Brothers," Opie declared proud as a peacock. "Best damn performers in the whole state of Wisconsin. My Grandma Betty is their manager, you know. They're coming to Chicago to meet up with us so we can start that band you were talking about. Wait until you meet them. They're absolutely terrific and a lot of fun too."

"Hold on there…not so fast," Probo shot back, getting his dander up. "I'm not some half-witted banjo player you picked up along the road. I don't jam with just anybody. I'm an accomplished artist, a world-class musician…it's top billing for me next time or nothing at all."

"No, no," Opie shot back. "You don't understand. The Brothers already have all the attention they can handle back home.

"That's why they're looking for someone to help take some of the pressure off. Why, only last year they were so exhausted from entertaining a bunch of groupies in the back of their van that they fell asleep with the engine running and had to be rushed to the hospital. They had just been pronounced dead of monoxide poisoning when suddenly they sat up, stared at the nurse standing alongside the gurney and exclaimed in perfect unison, 'Hey there babe…where'd you get them hooters?' That's the kind of keen-witted characters they are. Funny as hell. Identical twins, you know."

"Keen-witted, eh?" Probo murmured with a look of disdain. "Wait a minute…did you say…*groupies?*"

"You bet," the drummer responded, taking note of the elephant's sudden change of interest. "And I know they're going to be dying to meet you. People of your, er…*persuasion* are very popular back in Madapahadawanee. And remember, it *is* an election year. So if it's that young, Republican booty you have a taste for, there's plenty of it." Opie grinned that big, toothy smile of his that made him look like a mule. Opie liked mules…but then, he was a Democrat. Of course, no one had ever told him that the Party's symbol was that of a *donkey*, not a mule. "So what?" he would probably say. "I guess that means some of those politicians down in Washington will have to be a bit more careful when they fool around." Opie was smart that way.

"You say they like elephants?" inquired the pachyderm, following up on the drummer's remarks. "And, uh, what instruments did you say these Gornisht fellows play?"

"Instruments? Naw, they don't play any instruments," said the drummer, producing a toothpick out of nowhere and poking at his teeth. "They're moaners...they *moan*."

"What do you mean...*moan*?" Probo demanded, the impatience showing in his face.

"Well, my Grandma Betty can explain it better than I can. It's a bit like singing, I guess - only there are no words to it, just a bunch of sounds, the kind you wouldn't want to hear in a dark alley at night. People come from miles away just to see the twins perform. Those who can't travel stay at home and have the performance phoned in. I'm telling you, Probo, these guys are heavy breathers. It makes the girls go crazy."

Probo rolled his eyes in the direction of the gas station attendant and another man who were pushing Opie's truck off to the side. Opie watched them with tear-filled eyes as he continued with his story. "Believe me, Probo...the twins are really dark. When they get to making those weird sounds of theirs it's as if people fall into a trance or something. They get to drooling and stumbling all over the place - kind of like zombies at a hoe-down, you might say. You have to see it to believe it."

"Stumbling and drooling, eh?" said Probo, trying to stifle a laugh. "I think I know what you mean. I saw a bit of that myself as I was walking around the neighborhood earlier. In fact, there's some guy now, collapsed up against that lamppost, looking like he's about three sheets to the wind."

It wasn't Probo's fault that the former race horse and world-class stud had to be fixed.

"Him? Oh, he's just one of the locals," interjected the gas station attendant as he rejoined the pair. "He's probably beat to hell from standing around all day waiting for a bus. Public transportation really sucks in this town. Only last week some guy on the Wilson 'L' platform got so pissed off waiting for a train that when it finally arrived he threw himself under the wheels...just for the spite of it. It costs the city plenty to reroute the passengers...not to mention the mess they have to clean up."

"Yes, I know about spite," Probo said pensively, thinking back on that vengeful nag, Harry the Happy Gelding, who used to leave his special 'packages' hidden behind the bandstand where the elephant was sure to pass. It wasn't Probo's fault that the handsome lady-killer had to be fixed. *Someone* had to inform the old circus master that the pretty acrobats in their pink and yellow outfits weren't the *only* ones riding the trick ponies at night after the circus shut down. "And I'm not talking about the trained monkeys in their little fez hats," added the trumpet player, whispering in the master's ear...though he knew full well the frisky rascals enjoyed a romp around the track themselves every now and then. Of course, Probo didn't want to be known as a whistleblower, so he urged the senescent circus impresario not to bring his name into it. Unfortunately, word leaked out anyway. That's when the former race horse and world-class stud began to have it in for the dirty little snitch.

"Er...you say the girls really go crazy for these Gornisht characters?" Probo asked his fair-haired companion, his mind wandering back to the drummer's earlier comments. "You bet," Opie responded coyly, avoiding eye contact with his friend. "It's more than crazy. It's almost as if the twins put some kind of spell on them. No one is immune. Not men, not women…not even dogs and cats. I saw a bird once fall out of a tree while the twins were rehearsing in the yard. Actually, it didn't fall. It jumped. One day last year when I was home for a visit, this guy came into the club where the twins were performing. He was rotten drunk and waving a pistol, yelling about how he was going to shoot both of them dead. He was mad as hell because his sister had gotten pregnant by one of them, or so he claimed. Anyway, he wasn't in the place for more than a minute when the twins stepped onto the stage and began moaning, real slow and somber-like. Before you could say Jimmy Crack Corn the guy threw down the pistol, spun around on his boot heels and walked right out the door."

"Wait a minute!" Probo retorted angrily, setting his mule-faced companion back on his own well-worn heels. "What the hell you talking about? You just said that anyone who hears the twins perform loses all self-control and gets to stumbling around like some sort of zombie. So how is it that the fellow with the gun was able to maintain his composure and walk right out of the place without so much as a how-de-do?"

"Like I said…," replied the drummer, cool and confident as an IRS agent finding a two-dollar error in a ten-dollar tax return. "He came into the club stone-drunk and barely able to walk. When you're stumbling *already*, there ain't no place further to stumble *to*…so they just kind of cancel each other out, and you end up *falling straight!*"

4. Ain't Nobody Here that's Never Voted

"*Falling straight!* Unbelievable," Probo muttered to himself as he hurried down the street in search of the small hotel the man at the gas station had told him about. He knew of Opie's penchant for telling tall tales, and he doubted anything the Wisconsin kid had told him that day had an ounce of truth to it. "He's not so smart," Probo assured himself out loud as he passed a homeless man begging from a doorway. "He may be able to hustle everyone else, but he won't get a penny out of me." The beggar drew back into the doorway like a wilting flower.

Probo had promised his circus buddy he would return shortly and keep him company until his grandmother arrived. He at least owed him that. Meanwhile, he rambled along the avenue taking note of the boarded-up houses and abandoned two-flats, wondering what sort of future he might find in this unforgiving city. He soon arrived at the dingy, single-story structure with the rusty, hand-painted sign out front that read:

Zyg's Paradise
The "Jewel of Chicago"
Rooms nightly or by the week
Welcome 47th Chicago Livestock Exhibition Participants.

With its cheap, cinder block siding and corrugated roof the place looked more like a garage or converted storage facility than a place for visitors to the Windy City to park the kids while they took in the sights. But then, most Americans consider any place that has poor Mexicans turning down the beds at night and leaving free chocolates on the pillow to be the lap of luxury.

The desk clerk was a short, stocky man with a thick, red neck which he tried to conceal behind a high, dirty collar. He eyed Probo suspiciously as he entered the small, cluttered room that served as an office. A naked bulb swung freely from the ceiling, while a nearby fan wobbled on its axle rustling the yellow news clippings pasted to the wall announcing Roosevelt's re-election to yet another term. Here and there large specimens of perch and salmon glared down at the visitor - trophies no doubt taken from the nearby lake, though they had the distinct appearance of having been bludgeoned to death rather than reeled in on a line.

"I'd like a room for the night," Probo stammered, affecting a deep, phony voice the way teenagers do when trying to purchase alcohol. People often took him for being much younger than he was - no doubt part of the reason some folks called him *boy,* though it might also be due to the affection many still felt for him from the days when he accompanied his mother, the famous Molly, during her performances under the big top. Molly was known far and wide for her one-of-a-kind act in which she danced blindfolded around her trainer as he lay prostrate at her feet and her cuddly, long-eared two-year-old played *Yankee Doodle Dandy* on the kazoo. But those days were gone, and Probo tried not to think about them too much.

"This is Chicago, boy," said the man. "Ain't nobody here that's never voted."

"You from out of town, boy?" the man asked, sizing the elephant up and down as if he had come in to try on a suit. "Peanutville," Probo replied, casting a wary eye at an old sofa with a faded pattern of roses that lay collapsed in the corner like an untended grave. Its soiled cushions bore the imprint of something that apparently had died there and remained unmoved for ages. Over the faux mantelpiece hung the snarling, evil-looking head of some sort of animal…a small fox perhaps, or possibly a weasel. It glared at the circus lad with beady, red eyes that seemed to study his every move. When one of these objects lurched suddenly from its socket and fell to the floor, Probo's mind almost did the same. It rolled noisily across the wooden floorboards, coming to a stop against one of the elephant's big, flat feet. "Damn it!" shouted the desk clerk, rushing out from behind the service counter and making his way over to where the object lay. "I thought I had that fixed. Time I took that rotten thing out back and threw it in the alley. Let the neighborhood kids play with it."

The man kneeled down, wrapped his fist around what looked like a small, glass marble, examined it closely for a moment and placed it carefully in his pocket. "Peanutville, eh?" he repeated, slowly rising and making his way back to the seat behind the cash register. "Dang, that's Jimmie Carter Country. That means you must be a Democrat, right?" Probo pondered the question for a moment, then responded, "Well…I don't know. I've never really voted."

"Never voted?" the man cried out with a look of horror and dismay. "This is Chicago, boy. Ain't *nobody* here that's never voted. But don't worry, come election time I'll show you the ropes. I'm Zyg Zypltowvtz, the precinct captain hereabouts. You need anything...a new garbage can, a building permit, a parking ticket fixed...I'm your man. But listen, you need a room? I'll fix you up real good. Are you alone or, er, expecting someone else?"

"Just me," said Probo, shifting nervously on his feet. "How much will that cost?" The man hesitated, glancing up at the snarling head mounted above the mantelpiece as if he were awaiting some sort of a sign. All at once a second orb, identical to the first, shot from its decrepit host and tumbled to the floor. Again, the man with the thick, red neck ran over, stooped down and stuffed the object into his pants. "Son of a bitch," he grumbled, once more turning his attention to the sharp-toothed oracle leering blindly from the wall. This time he seemed to find the answer he'd been searching for. "Twenty dollars," he blurted out. "Yes, twenty dollars...that ought to do it. That will get you a room with a nice double bed and a private bath. And you're in luck, because I just happen to have one available. The guy who's in there now should have been out hours ago. I think I'll go kick his ass."

"Uh, well that won't be necessary," Probo insisted, looking a bit nonplussed. "Actually, do you have something a bit...*cheaper*?" As the last word sprang from his mouth, Probo thought he could hear the sound of teeth gnashing somewhere behind him. "Cheaper?" the man repeated, looking a bit perplexed. He reached deep into his pocket and began toying with the tiny, red balls he found there. A slight hint of ecstasy played across his lips. "Well, for ten bucks I can give you one of our...*specials*. It doesn't come with a mattress or any other accommodations, but we do provide a supply of fresh straw daily. We get a lot of requests for those, especially when there's a convention in town. Of course, we've had some problems with the city health inspectors, but a few tickets to the ward organization's annual fund raiser usually takes care of that. All the corned beef and cabbage you can eat. Free drinks too. Most of the local officials are there, shaking hands and schmoozing in the corridors. Problem was, there was this one inspector who didn't much care for corned beef. Can you imagine that? What an asshole! Anyway, I arranged for him to sit in on one of our shootings. That seemed to satisfy him, and he went away happy."

"You had a shooting here?" Probo cried out with alarm. "What...?" the man echoed with a quizzical look. "Oh...yea, we get those too. But I was referring to this film crew that comes around every so often to shoot a, uh, documentary here...if you know what I mean." Probo wasn't sure he wanted to know what the man with the lascivious grin meant. He recalled the time some people came to Peanutville to shoot a film about circus life. They wandered around sticking their cameras into all the tents and cages, intruding upon everyone's privacy as if they were nothing more than a bunch of...well, animals, with no feelings of their own. When the production finally appeared on television some months later several of the red-bottomed rhesus monkeys that had been in heat at the time of the shooting threw themselves from the high wire...just for the shame of it all.

"They just film the stuff here," said the desk clerk as he sorted through the day's receipts. "The voice-overs are done up in

Wisconsin…at some studio near Green Bay I think. They hire young college gals looking to make some money and teach them to scream and holler by sending them to Packer games. That's why in so many of these films you see these babes rolling around with their keisters in the air, yelling things like *'Come on…come on, you son of a bitch. Move that pigskin! Put your shoulder into it.'* Frankly, I never watch the stuff. These women today are too aggressive for my taste. Say, you *are* a Bears fan, aren't you?" Probo thought about the despised anteater with the severed leg, white and shiny as an elephant's tusk - and a smile came to his face. "Sure, I like bears," he answered with a grin.

"Great! I can get you tickets for next season's opener, if you're interested," said the man with the thick, red neck and the tiny balls jangling in his pocket. "Meanwhile, you'd better make your mind up about the room. We've got a convention of newspaper reporters and TV journalists coming through here this weekend. They get like animals once they start drinking…and those *Ten* dollar rooms go fast."

As Probo wrestled with his decision, his attention was drawn to a huge mole on the precinct captain's neck. He had seen a walnut that size once…so big that a squirrel nearly gagged on it and had to abandon it where it lay. "Must bring in a lot of votes, though," he thought to himself. "People really go for that sort of thing back along the midway."

5. Dachshund Slippers

The Gornisht twins huddled across the table from Probo, shoulder to shoulder, cheek to jowl - their identical features merging in the dim light of the restaurant into a single, hideous expression. Each of the outrageously garbed figures wore a leather patch strung across one eye just at the point where their shaggy manes came together, leaving the two 'good' eyes they shared between them leering back from the outer parameters of an incredibly wide smirk. Probo had the distinct impression of sitting across from a hammerhead shark. Moments later, a third head appeared as a casually dressed woman slid her chair up to the table and introduced herself to the trumpet player with a soft, seductive smile. "I'm sorry to keep you waiting," she entreated in a singsong voice that sounded as if she had a bird in her throat. "I left something in the van." She had the wild and feral look of a flower-child who had been raised by wolves...in her late sixties perhaps, with coarse, unmanageable hair, grey with occasional streaks of blond running through it as if to defy the ravages of time. Large pupils, floating like dark moons above an emerald-green sea, stared back at the elephant, while lips warm and inviting as a Valentine's Day kiss seemed to ask, "Good evening, sir...is there *anything* I can get for you?" Probo was stunned. *This* was Opie's grandmother?

43

The hammerhead's broad, sardonic smirk melted into an even wider grin at the sight of Probo's consternation. Long rows of uncommonly white teeth gleamed back at the elephant, giving him reason to suspect that if there were a Cheshire cat to be found anywhere on the premises, this monster had already devoured it, even if it were *not* on the menu. A large cockroach scurrying along the floor caught Probo's attention and disappeared into a nearby crevice. An emaciated, grim-faced waitress with cadaverous red hair shuffled by, threw three dog-eared menus on the table and hurried off. The cockroach, sensing that the coast was clear, emerged a moment later with three or four companions in tow. Probo felt his stomach turn. All the coffee he had consumed while awaiting the Wisconsin group's arrival didn't help much either. During that time the two circus buddies swapped stories and took turns guessing at the red-headed woman's age. Probo estimated it to be somewhere between that of Moses and Methuselah, while his freckle-faced companion said with no uncertainty that he had seen the woman somewhere before...in a museum exhibit perhaps, during a sixth-grade field trip to see the mummies.

"Probo...this is my grandmother, Betty," said Opie as he leaned across the table. And these are the Gornisht twins, Buck and Howdy. Everybody...this is Probo, the trumpet player I worked with back in Peanutville." Opie looked rather pleased with himself for having carried off these introductions with such aplomb. Betty was beaming like a school girl on prom night. The shark said nothing, but simply stared at the elephant as if he were some morsel dangling from a hook. Probo tried to force a smile, which succeeded only in making him look all the more like a piece of bait with a death wish.

"Probo, eh?" Betty repeated, rolling the name around on her tongue as if it were a cherry cordial she was about to bite into. Probo felt the soft, chewy caramel at the center of his being go limp as the woman once more threw a seductive smile his way, adding in that singsong voice of hers, "Yes, I like that. I think it will look great on the colorful posters I'm thinking of designing. I can see it now: *Probo, the Bull Elephant and his Golden Trumpet, Straight From the Jungles of Pago Pago.* What do you think, Opie?"

"I like it, grandma. It has a certain...panache to it."

"Watch it!" the woman snapped sharply, causing the Wisconsin lad to draw back into his seat. "I'll have none of that filthy language of yours around our guest." Brushing her hair coyly to one side, the boy's grandmother turned to the wide-eyed elephant and cooed, "So tell me...what's a nice, clean-cut fellow like you doing in a place like this?" Probo glanced at his red-faced circus buddy and began to stammer. All the defenses he had amassed in anticipation of meeting the former 'Mistress of the Midway' - as some folks called her - suddenly vanished. With some difficulty he managed to eek out a response. "Well, actually I'm here hoping to hook up with a decent band and make a name for myself."

"Is that so?" said the woman, tossing the two-headed creature seated at her side a furtive glance. "And what, if may I ask, is wrong with the name you currently have? Probo...isn't it? As I said a moment ago, I think it will look fine on the promotional materials I'm planning on designing."

Probo swallowed hard and stared down at his coffee. "Uh, no…perhaps I didn't make myself clear. What I mean to say is, my intention is to establish myself as an important artist here in a city where people will truly appreciate me."

"Oh, so it's *appreciation* that you want! What a coincidence! The twins and I have been talking for some time about coming to Chicago and picking up on some of that big city appreciation ourselves. No one appreciates strangers like Chicagoans. Why, I hear they're so full of appreciation they treat each other like strangers just for the joy of it. Speaking of appreciation…I'm sure Opie has told you about all the attention the twins have been getting back in Wisconsin. More than they can handle, actually. That's why we think it's time to move on. Take the show on the road, as they say. Besides, there are some people looking for these two back home."

"Yea, I hear that guy's sister had twins," spouted the drummer proud as a pumpkin and looking as if he'd just become an uncle. "Shut up, Opie," the youth's grandmother demanded as she reached for a menu. "You know damn well the twins had nothing to do with that. It's just a case of, er, mistaken identity." The shark glared threateningly at the grinning pumpkin, its twin jaws locked tighter than a noose.

"Anyway, back to why we're here. The twins and I have long been thinking that bringing some new members into the group would be just the thing to take the act in a new direction. I think there's an opportunity here to create the kind of sound that will make these big city audiences stand up and take notice."

46

"Yes, well...," said Probo, glancing at his watch. It was getting late and he was concerned that the room he'd put the deposit on back at the hotel might not be waiting for him. He could kick himself for not asking for a receipt. "To tell you the truth," he told the woman studying him intently from the opposite side of the table, "your offer is very inviting, but I really wasn't planning on..."

"Why, of course you were!" the woman retorted. "We all were. That's why the minute Opie telephoned and told me that you and he were in Chicago, we loaded up the van and headed for the highway. I don't have to tell you, but Wang is very excited about this. He's looking forward to meeting you." Probo had the curious feeling that something had just flown by his head. "Wang?" he inquired meekly, wondering if perhaps someone else was supposed to join them at the restaurant. "And who, if you don't mind my asking, is this Wang?" Betty reached into her handbag and pulled out a pack of Luckies. Fumbling with her lighter, she left the elephant dangling in the middle of the conversation like a fish on a hook. This, of course, sent the hammerhead into a tizzy. "Wang is my ex-husband," she finally answered with a tremble in her voice. "He runs a little place not far from here that serves Chinese food and such. And he's thrilled at the prospect of featuring a live band on weekends to attract the crowds. It's an idea he and I have been kicking around for some time. Now, with you and Opie on board, that will be possible. We figure it will be great for business and at the same time help the twins here get a foothold into the Chicago scene."

Probo had the distinct impression of sitting across from a hammerhead shark.

"Your ex-husband, eh?" Probo chuckled, looking the twins' manager up and down. "That's interesting. I never met anyone who was married to a Chinese person...except another Chinese of course. But then, I never met a Chinese who was married to someone who wasn't...Chinese, that is." Opie, who had been listening attentively to the conversation, glanced at his grandmother, then leaned back smugly in his chair...content to know he wasn't the only idiot at the table.

"Chinese? Wang's not Chinese," the woman retorted. He's an Okie...from Muskogee, if you really care to know. He bought the restaurant a few years ago from some Armenian fellow who taught him the business. The man's English wasn't too good, so if you see items like 'Pimp with Oyster Sauce' or 'Tasty Stir-fried Poodles' on the menu...don't be concerned. Wang plans on having it reprinted. But as I was saying...he's completely on board with us and has agreed to close down the restaurant for a few days so we can begin rehearsing for the big event this Saturday."

"This Saturday? But today is already Wednesday, Grandma. Are you sure that's enough time?" Once again, the lad's grandmother threw him a reproachful look as the shark, ever watchful for any sort of unwarranted behavior, snarled and bared its teeth. This caused Probo to draw back suddenly, knocking a glass of water from the table. The sound of it shattering caused the creature to lurch, the two 'good' eyes on either side of its strangely conjoined head narrowing into slits as if under the control of a single, guiding intelligence. Opie sat silently with scarcely concealed glee as he waited for his grandmother to unleash her wrath on his unsuspecting friend. Maybe now, the elephant would regret not lending him the money he'd asked for. But the woman with the singsong voice and hard-as-nails demeanor simply ignored the incident and smiled quietly to herself as if lost in some faraway world of her own. "I'll greet the customers as they arrive," she giggled, sounding like Shirley Temple on one of her Good Ship Lollypop highs. "It's time I got into one of those cute little cocktail waitress outfits again. I haven't done that in years. According to Zyg, there should be no problem getting a temporary liquor license by the weekend."

Zyg! The name had an ominous ring to it, like the tolling of church bells on the day of an execution. Probo took a deep breath before he spoke. "Uh, excuse me. May I ask…who is this Zyg you're referring to?" A wave of paranoia washed across his brain as his medulla oblongata went into overdrive, sending a torrent of blood rushing to all parts of his body. The shark, always on the scent, sat up in its seat(s) and glared at the offender as if a side of mutton had just dropped from the sky. Probo recalled Opie's earlier remark regarding how much fun the twins could be. If hanging with these characters was fun, Probo reflected, then inviting Charles Manson up your apartment for a dose of laughing gas and a round of Russian roulette must be a fucking orgy.

"Zyg's my cousin," said Betty, responding to Probo's question with an uneasy glance. "He runs a small hotel of sorts here in Chicago. Lovely place, or so I've been told. I've never actually seen it. Why do you ask?" Probo stared into his cup to escape the hammerhead's sharp, unerring gaze. "Oh, no reason in particular," he said, studying his reflection in the coffee's deep, unfathomable depths. "I think I met him earlier today while I was looking for a place to stay."

"Met him? *You met him?*" Betty exclaimed, her pupils growing wide as black holes at the center of the galaxy, drawing in any last hopes Probo might have of extricating himself from his present company and making it back to the safety of the hotel. But then, even if the room he'd reserved was still waiting for him, he wasn't at all certain how this Zyg fellow fit into the picture. "Well, I hope you won't be *too* disappointed...," said the woman somewhat threateningly as her attention shifted to the pale-faced drummer with the yellow shock of hair, "but I've taken the liberty of arranging for us to all stay at Wang's for a few days while the band prepares for Saturday night's performance." The shark grinned wildly. The side of mutton felt a flush of blood rising to his head. Probo struggled to find the words to carry him through the moment as he imagined a lush, high-rise apartment with a big Jacuzzi overlooking the nearby lake. "Hmmm, sounds interesting," he ventured sheepishly. "How many bedrooms does it have?"

"Bedrooms? What bedrooms? Wang lives at the YMCA. I'm talking about the restaurant," Betty retorted. "There's a small room off the back where you and Opie can sleep. I'll crash in the dining room, while the twins here can camp out in the van. I've brought some blankets along, so we'll all be comfortable. It's not quite the paradise Zyg's place is supposed to be, but it will do...and save you a few dollars besides. What do you say?"

Before Probo could respond his attention was drawn to the gruesome-looking duo on the far side of the table. He had never seen Siamese twins before and like most people found their appearance rather unsettling. But something was happening now. Little by little, imperceptibly at first, their shaggy manes of hair which had been hopelessly tangled together began to draw apart...separating as it were like dark strands of chromosomes in a slowly dividing cell. Moments later the process was complete, leaving the monstrous hammerhead nowhere to be found and in its place a pair of hideous one-headed clones, indistinguishable from one another except for the black patches strung across opposite sides of their heads. Probo sat frozen with horror, then shuddered and looked away.

Betty flagged down the waitress and ordered from the menu while the two newly-created organisms seated at her side browsed through some magazines they produced out of nowhere and began reading as calmly as if they were waiting for a manicure. Once again Probo stared into his coffee, seeking comfort in its dark, imponderable depths. His mind drifted back to what Betty had told him about her plans for the group. He liked the idea of performing in a Chinese restaurant. It reminded him of a film he'd seen - one of those old Charlie Chan flicks set back in the days when Shanghai was full of mystery and intrigue. There was this fancy nightclub full of rich Chinese businessmen who spoke with a British accent (or was it the other way around?), sipping gin and tonic and listening to a small jazz orchestra while beautiful women in tight, silky dresses slid seductively across their laps. It was the romantic image of a bygone age that had long resonated in the impressionable lad's mind. Now, here was an opportunity for Probo to see his fantasies played out right in front of him while cheering crowds toyed with their tea and chop-sticks and urged the band on. Just think, he reflected – people might come all the way from China to see what it's about...*Chinese* people, with beautiful women dressed in tight, sexy dresses just looking for a nice, big lap to slide into. Then too, there was all that talk about groupies. It sure wouldn't hurt to be known as the *bull* - as Betty had suggested - when those hot, young babes started coming around. Screw that 'boy' crap. Yea, he could go for that, thought the elephant. Maybe here at last was the break he'd been waiting for. According to Opie the Gornisht twins had a big following back in Wisconsin. It wouldn't take long for word to get around that they were appearing on stage with a world-class trumpet player. People would come from far and wide just to see the group perform and get down to drooling and stumbling...or whatever it was that folks did in Wisconsin on a Saturday night.

Probo glanced up from his coffee. The twins had returned to their former incarnation as the snub-nosed predator nature undoubtedly intended them to be. Probo was impressed. He had never seen detachable twins before. "Gee," he thought. "What wonders modern science can achieve. Maybe the medicine I'm on will help improve my eyesight after all." A lull in the conversation, meanwhile, had settled over the group, causing the self-conscious pachyderm to feel a bit unnerved. Clearly such insecurities derived from the old adage about the 'elephant in the room' - a line that people seemed to drop a lot whenever Probo was around. The tension soon became palpable, more than the circus lad could endure. Finally, he blurted out, "So tell me, Betty...what's the name of this restaurant we're talking about?" Betty laughed. "That's an easy one. Right now it's called *Wang's,* but I'm hoping our esteemed host will agree with my suggestion that we change the name to *Wang's Dang Noodles.* Has a nice ring to it, don't you think?" Probo reflected for a moment, then, with a grin responded, "Pretty clever...I assume you got the idea from that recording of *Wang Dang Doodle* that Howling Wolf made famous some years ago."

"What the hell you talking about?" the woman snapped sharply, the singsong in her voice sounding more like roadkill with feathers. All at once the hammerhead began reeling wildly like some wind-up doll gone murderously berserk. "Forgive me," said Betty, regaining control of herself and assuming a more gentle tone. "It brings back painful memories." She raised her hand and the thing reeling crazily at her side came to a halt. Wiping a tear from her eye, she continued, "Fact is, the idea for the name came from an incident that took place the last time my late husband, Sturgis, and I were together. We were hanging out in that backwoods cabin of his, cooking up some breakfast and listening to the radio - when all of a sudden Stu's favorite song came on the air...a funky little tune called *Back Door Man*. 'Stu!' I shouted, 'I'll be wang dang doodled...they're playing your song.' That Sturgis was the best back door man I ever knew. You could be sitting in your kitchen, peeling potatoes or something, when all of a sudden...bam!...there he was, standing all hot and heavy and breathing down on you. Stu was an outdoorsman, you see. One hell of a sharpshooter. Almost never missed. Loved to hunt with those old dogs of his along, one on each leg. That's how he was able to move so soft and quiet-like. Beautiful things...still had the heads on them, too."

"I beg your pardon?" said Probo with a dazed and vacant expression. "The heads...?"

"Stu's Dachshund moccasins. More like slippers actually. He made them himself, right from the pelts. Like I said, with those old dogs of his on each foot a jackrabbit couldn't have heard him coming. Anyway, I was in the mood to bake some cookies, so I sent Stu over to Lucius Pine's place to borrow a cup of sugar from his wife, Candy. Lucius was a good-for-nothing who spent most of his time drinking and lying around the house...that is, when he wasn't out fishing. Candy was standing at the kitchen sink rinsing out some ladies garments when Sturgis slipped up behind her, real quiet like, and said, 'Hey there, sweetheart...how's about some sugar?' Sturgis called everybody sweetheart. Well, Candy let out a scream and Lucius, who was home at the time, came running into the kitchen, threw open the refrigerator door and bashed Sturgis in the head with a frozen carp. But that's not what killed him. Stu was a diabetic, and he died of insulin shock walking the five miles to the hospital with the carp sticking out of his head. Doctor Savage said Stu was the toughest man he ever met."

An awkward silence once again descended upon the group, adding to the elephant's discomfort. No one said a thing. Probo glanced up to find Opie staring straight at him with that mule-faced grin of his. A couple of cockroaches creeping across the table stopped frozen in their tracks, sensing the presence of the nearby waitress. No one said a thing. Probo glanced up to find Opie staring straight at him with that mule-faced grin of his. A couple of cockroaches creeping across the table stopped frozen in their tracks, sensing the presence of the nearby waitress. No one said a thing. Probo glanced up to find Opie staring straight at him with that mule-faced grin of his. No one said a thing...

"Damn!" thought the elephant, rubbing his eyes. "I hate it when that happens." What Probo didn't realize was that *'that'* had been happening more and more in recent months - ever since he'd started taking his medicine, a sizable dose of which he had consumed shortly before the Wisconsin group's arrival. As on prior occasions strange voices were tripping through his brain, offering up bits of small talk or witty repartee he might use to impress whatever company he was in or get a stalled conversation back on track. Apparently those same voices thought the present moment perfectly opportune for leading the addlebrained elephant into one of his infamous gaffs. "You know, I was wondering...," he began, glancing at his mule-faced buddy and turning to Betty. "Just out of curiosity...which of these former husbands of yours, Wang or Sturgis, would be Opie's grandfather?"

"Opie's *grandfather?"* What do you think I am, boy?" the woman exploded, sending the shark into another one of its frenzies. "Listen, I received a measly twenty-six dollars a month in those days to take that kid in. Do you think it was easy, what with Stu dead and me working long hours on the carnival circuit?" All at once the shapely, green-eyed carny stood up and leaned threateningly across the table, causing the dumbstruck elephant to recoil in terror. Then she whispered, soft and seductive, right in his ear, "I don't know if you've noticed...but that boy has spent too many hours riding around on the bumper cars without a helmet." Probo cast a furtive glance at the slender youth with his long legs stretched out across the aisle as he studied the cadaverous-looking waitress from behind. "Yes, I know exactly what you mean," Probo confided as Betty sank back into her seat with a smug look of approval.

6. Hogs and Hearses

Betty fumbled with the crackers, crumbling them into her soup while the shark sat quietly, scanning the premises in hopes that something dead might float by. All that materialized was the decrepit waitress shuffling over to the table to bring Betty her sandwich. Probo stared off into the distance contemplating his future, or at least that particular version of it which Betty had so effortlessly planted in his mind. He was eager to ask her some questions, but fearful that the least misstep might unleash the horror sitting beside her. As usual, lulls in the conversation which Probo found so unnerving compelled him to speak. "Everything you've told me about your plans for the group is, of course, very interesting, but frankly I'm still not clear as to what this moaning thing is all about. I really don't think it's something I can...."

"Think?" the woman sputtered, nearly choking on her food. Pushing the plate away she signaled the twins who, sensing that something had happened but not quite knowing what, looked ready to pounce. "You don't have to think," she said sharply before catching herself and reverting to her usual voice, sweet and seductive as the cookies she baked. The creature had already begun rising threateningly from its seat(s), but another wave from Betty's well-manicured hand and it withdrew like a beaten dog.

"It's not all that complicated," the dog's master continued. "I'm sure Opie has explained it to you…but perhaps I can elaborate."

Sitting straight up in her chair, Betty assumed a formal demeanor which caused the sleepy-eyed drummer and the equally languorous twins to snap to attention. It appeared as if some important lecture were about to begin. Probo wondered whether he should take notes. "As I'm sure you know," the speaker began, "there are numerous ways in which music can be used to enhance or manipulate a person's moods. Take the movies for example. Have you ever seen one of those old prison films from the '30s and '40s, the ones with the black guy leaning through the bars of his cell, singing *Nobody Knows the Trouble I've Seen,* while the white guy - who's innocent of course - makes his way down the corridor toward the death chamber? Let me ask you something: have you ever wondered why the people who made those films didn't have the condemned man sing the song himself? I'll tell you why…because they knew damn well that white people can't sing the blues for shit. Am I making myself clear, Probo?"

Probo wasn't sure what to say. The hammerhead was observing him closely through half-closed eyes, awaiting his response. The silence was deafening. Finally the elephant lad spoke. "I think so, Betty. I seem to recall seeing the sequel to that film in which the condemned man receives a last-minute reprieve from the governor. That same black guy was in it, laughing and dancing and jumping around in his cell, singing *Happy Days Are Here Again* as the white guy was led out of prison - a free man, into the loving arms of his wife. It was very touching."

58

"Uh…yes," said Betty, "but the point I'm trying to make is that when people are depressed or feeling down they usually want *someone else* to express those emotions for them. Sure, everyone hums a happy little tune now and then, while taking a shower or cruising in their car, but how many people sit around singing *Gloomy Sunday* to themselves when they've lost their job or their pet gerbil has died? Most folks under such circumstances prefer to put some sad music on the radio or head out to a nightclub to hear some blues. And that's where the twins come in. Nobody sings the blues the way they do, be they young or old, black or white. And do you know why? Because the twins reach out to everyone, rich and poor alike."

"I'm afraid you've lost me, Betty," Probo said meekly. "I thought the twins were into moaning. Moaning isn't singing. It doesn't even use words."

"Who needs words?" Betty countered. "Music takes many forms. Hasn't anyone ever come up to you after a performance and commented on how you made that instrument of yours 'sing'? You get my meaning? Listen, everyone knows the blues deals with themes such as not having enough food to put on the table, or having your best friend's wife cheat on you, or being born under a bad sign…that sort of thing. But what about the guy who can't meet the payments on his new Mercedes and is at risk of having it repossessed? What about the guy whose stocks dropped half a point and he has to sell off his summer home in Palm Springs? What about the poor woman who is beside herself because the bitch next door showed up at the governor's inauguration wearing the same one-of-a-kind designer dress she just paid a fortune for?

"I'm talking about people who die with their jewelry on Probo, not those who pawn it for a loaf of bread. What about them? Who's going to sing *their* sad songs? Blind Willie Rockefeller?"

"Blind Willie who?" the elephant stammered as Betty pulled a cigarette from her bag and lit it. "Let me put it this way," she continued, "The blues is about a certain kind of feeling, whether you moan it, groan it, sing it or wail it on some guitar. Everyone in Chicago knows that."

"Well, you got me there," Probo conceded with a show of enthusiasm meant to please everyone at the table. The shark, however, wasn't impressed. It wasn't even listening for that matter, having nodded off with its eyes wide open - or at least the two that Probo knew about. Opie, too, was slumped in his seat, about to slide onto the floor.

"Not to change the subject," Betty insisted, "but did Opie tell you how the twins got their start, performing at county fairs, funerals and the like? Why, you couldn't have a decent hog sale or burial in Racine County without the twins there to do their thing. Where I come from people take it pretty hard when their prize pig is auctioned off to the slaughter house or a loved one dies. Plenty of times I've seen folks sitting around the cemetery, pitching pennies or playing canasta - just waiting for the twins show up. Once they arrived and began chanting those dark incantations of theirs, friends and family of the deceased could finally release all that pent-up emotion and get down to some serious grieving. My God, it was a sight to behold! Needless to say it wasn't long before clubs and show lounges throughout the area were clamoring for the twins to get up and perform on stage. After all, where else other than a funeral do you find so many people sitting around crying to themselves, if not your local tavern? By the time the twins got their new stage act together there wasn't a lonely or depressed soul this side of Bucyrus who didn't try to drown his or her troubles in a couple of beers at one of their shows. The club owners were ecstatic...that is, until some of the customers managed to drown what little was left of their grey matter in a glass of vodka or a bottle of vermouth, resulting in their dropping down dead in the middle of the dance floor."

Probo listened attentively to Betty's presentation as Opie and the hammerhead nodded off at her side. Betty appeared not to notice but kept on talking, puffing away at her cigarette and blowing smoke rings in the air. "As I was saying, it wasn't long before the twins were drawing huge crowds, thrilling audiences with the same kind of morose, deathbed inspired grunts and groans that made them popular in the first place. But with customers dropping like flies and slitting their wrists in the rest rooms we decided to dispense with the darker aspects of the performance and lighten things up a bit...do something a bit more cheerful like those catchy, upbeat tunes you hear in New Orleans funeral processions. You know, stuff like *Taps* and *Just a Closer Walk with Thee*. Not something to drink yourself to death over, but enough to make you want to come back and try again. We figured that would make the club owners happy and help sell plenty of booze besides. That's what the music business is all about, isn't it? Making money, becoming famous, getting laid...getting laid out on a nice, cool slab somewhere with a needle in your arm. That's showbiz, American style. So what do you say, Probo...are you with us?"

Betty's long-winded presentation apparently had been too much for the rest of the group. The twins had dozed off completely, while Opie was curled up on the floor sobbing and murmuring something about his long lost father. Betty, looking as if she had just finished a satisfying hour of coitus, leaned back in her chair taking slow, deliberate drags on her cigarette. The waitress came by and poured Probo another cup of coffee. As she bent over he noticed huge flakes of dandruff peeling from her scalp and a fresh coat of varnish holding her henna-colored, 3,000 year old bouffant in place. Once again a wave of paranoia raced across his brain uprooting whatever vestiges of sanity he might have clung to as the fast-moving tsunami washed away cherished images of mother and home. In their place stood the horrendous image of a gigantic clown, laughing and screeching and stomping around within the narrow confines of the elephant's confused and muddled mind. Everywhere it went it wreaked havoc, causing Probo to fear that any moment the raging maniac's size-forty shoes might rip through the very canvas of his dream, leaving the dreamer himself torn and deflated and lying in the dust like an empty suit of clothes. Probo started, returning to his senses as someone called his name. Looking up, he saw the twins slouched in their seats, snoring lightly with both eyes open. Suddenly one of them winked at him, sending the trumpet player reeling off into the faraway, hallucinatory world he'd just emerged from. But instead of finding himself face to face with giant clowns, he found himself back on that fatal afternoon when he and his mother shared the spotlight for the very last time. There they were, Probo humming out melodies on his little kazoo, Molly stepping ever so

*The horrendous image of a gigantic clown rose up
within the elephant's confused and muddled mind.*

lightly around her trainer's head. It all came to an end when some prankster threw a firecracker into the ring, causing the older animal to lose her footing. That's what led to Molly's so-called early retirement. Normally they destroy an animal when it's involved in the death of a human; but as it turned out the local sheriff held a considerable interest in the Peanutville Circus, so he simply took the perpetrator - some moronic sixteen-year-old with a Bobby Vee haircut - out back and shot him instead.

"Well, I guess I'm with you," Probo stammered as exhaustion from the long day's ordeal finally overtook him. Even his paranoia decided to call it a night, satisfied that there was more than enough material here to send the elephant screaming from the rafters on some future occasion.

"Terrific! Then we're on," said the group's manager, no less fatigued from her lengthy efforts to win over the reluctant trumpet player. Despite having given in to the woman's demands, Probo took considerable pride in knowing that he had not surrendered easily to her persuasions. Elephants can be quite stubborn - another reason Probo continued using the sweet-smelling drug that produced such peculiar side effects each time he used it. It had cost him a pretty penny and he wasn't about to throw it all away. "Oh, just one thing," he announced boldly, glancing back at Betty as he reached for his suitcase. "I don't want to look like some sort of clown up there on stage. If it turns out that these Gornisht characters can't carry a tune or keep up with the time changes, I'm moving on." Betty smiled reassuringly. "Fear not, my friend. You're not in Peanutville. You're dealing with people who have been at this game a long time. In the end I think you'll be pleasantly surprised."

"Game? What game? What sort of surprise?" Probo stammered, looking less sure of himself than he had a moment before. The woman with the emerald green eyes simply smiled and said, "Oh, by the way...don't worry about any deposit you may have put down on a room at Zyg's. I'll get it back for you the next time I see him." As she stood up and snatched the check from the table, she kicked the chair out from under one of the twins, sending both of them spilling onto the floor. The weepy-eyed drummer, thus alerted, scrambled to his feet. "Let's get out of here," the boy's grandmother demanded. "It's getting late, and Wang is waiting for us. Opie, you drive the van. These fuckers are out of it."

As Probo followed Betty from the restaurant he spotted a small tattoo at the back of her neck, nearly hidden by her long, grey locks. Two words... **'Bad Boy'**...etched into her milk-white skin by some flawless hand. As if by instinct the former carny reached behind her, brushed her hair back across the aging scar and hurried on.

7. The 200-Pound Little Dutch Boy

The next morning Probo and Opie awoke to find themselves spread out on the floor of a spare room at the back of Wang's restaurant that opened onto the main dining area via a sliding door. Wiping the sleep from his eyes, Probo peered into the adjacent chamber, dazzled at the sight of painted dragons and decorative pagodas festooning the walls. Paper lanterns dangled from the ceiling, while a squat, fat-bellied Buddha watched from the corner with an inscrutable grin. Probo stepped back from the doorway to admit a tall, slightly stooped man carrying a fresh tray of pastries and a steaming pot of tea. He appeared to be a good deal older than his former spouse, whom he smiled at warmly as she entered the room a moment later. Considering his age he looked pretty well preserved except for the cheap toupee he sported and a trim, dark beard, both of which looked as if they could use another coat of shoe polish. These, together with the conspicuous swagger he affected as he walked across the room, gave him the appearance of a six-foot Munchkin on a seven-day bender. Setting the tray on a nearby table he greeted his visitors with a hearty laugh. "Ni hau, one and all. Ni hau. That's Chinese for 'how are you?' Tea anyone?"

"Thanks," said Opie, inspecting the pastries in an attempt

to determine what sort of filling each one had. "Knee-how to you. Sorry if I wasn't very talkative when I came in last night. I was pretty beat. I assume you've met Probo here. He and I worked together back when I was with the circus."

"Ah yes, the trumpet player," the man with the ten-dollar hairpiece remarked somewhat sarcastically. "Betty always did have a thing for horn players," he added, staring accusingly at the grey-haired woman sitting unresponsively in a corner, sipping at her tea. Without further comment the grim-faced Munchkin stepped over to a nearby window, turned around suddenly and cast a suspicious eye on the elephant. All at once the atmosphere in the room grew tense. "Uh, it's a pleasure to meet you, Mr. Wang," Probo said awkwardly as the sweat ran down his collar. "It's very kind of you to welcome us to your little, er, pagoda here." Receiving no response, the circus lad glanced down at the huge clogs the man was wearing and added, somewhat jokingly, "What's with the wooden shoes? Been to Holland lately?"

"Holland?" the man exploded with an indignant tone that made all six hairs on the elephant's head stand up on end. "Holland?" he repeated, throwing Betty a look that seemed to ask *Who the fuck is this guy?* Without further comment he stalked across the room, his wooden shoes beating against the floorboards like angry hammers, and stuffed a handful of pastries into his mouth in an apparent effort to stifle some impending outburst. "Hell no, I haven't been to Holland!" he sputtered in an obvious failure at this attempt. "I wear these because of all the crap I have to wade around in each day. Let me ask you something *Mister Trumpet Player.* You've never worked in a restaurant, have you?

"No, I can see not. Well, let me tell you…people can be real pigs, especially when it comes to Chinese food, what with everyone passing the various dishes around and sampling from each of them with those tiny serving spoons we give them. Half of it ends up on the floor, and guess who has to clean it! I still haven't had a chance to mop up from yesterday. Some son of a bitch dribbled lobster sauce all over one of the chairs. Frankly Betty, I don't know how you could sleep out there with all that filth around you. For all you know it might bring rats…BIG ONES!"

The Gornisht twins shambled in looking more dead than alive - which wasn't particularly unusual for them. They helped themselves to refreshments and took up positions against the wall like a couple of sentries. Wang greeted them with scarcely a nod, to which they responded in kind. It hadn't occurred to Probo that these three were perhaps not that well acquainted. After a few moments of silence one of the twins addressed Betty in a deep, strangely affected voice that any respectable mortician would give his mother's eye teeth for. "There's space in one of the corners to set up the drums and equipment if we move a few tables around," he declared without the least show of enthusiasm. It was the first time Probo had heard either of the pair speak, though he couldn't say which one it was. He was content simply to have avoided any direct conversation with the hideous creature of the night before. "There's a pile of lumber and some old pallets out back that we can use to build a bandstand," Wang interjected, gesturing toward the window. "It may prove too small, however, to accommodate our hefty friend here," he added, glancing in Probo's direction as he seated himself alongside his former wife. The twins looked up from their tea and pastries and leered at the elephant as if

68

to say, "Yes, Tiny Tim…that *is* the finest Christmas goose anyone's ever seen." Probo cringed and stared out the window into the passageway beyond. Glancing at his watch, he noted that it was time for his medication. Excusing himself on some pretense or other, he located the door leading to the alley where rows of canisters piled high with the week's accumulation of trash graced the air with their incomparable scent. Stenciled across each of these, as if by the hand of some emotionally challenged seven-year-old, were the words 'COMPLIMENTS OF ZYG Z. VOTE DEMOCRATIC'.

"Geez," thought Probo, reaching into his suitcase and feeling around for the pocketbook-sized pouch he kept tucked away between his socks and underwear. "You could lead a herd of skunks through here and no one would notice." By the time he rejoined the others Wang and Betty were chatting happily away about their plans for the weekend and how they would accommodate the huge crowd they were expecting. Opie was exploring the side door that led to the kitchen, hoping to find something more to eat. Suddenly the restaurant owner leapt from his seat, raised a cup of tea to his lips and shouted, "L'chaim! Here's to success." Everyone in the room responded, "L'chaim"…except the Gornisht twins that is, though Probo thought he saw one of them throw a wink in the bearded man's direction. But he couldn't be sure.

After washing up in the small restroom situated just behind the kitchen, Opie and the twins set about unloading the van, carrying in loudspeakers and other equipment, along with the drums they'd salvaged from Opie's truck the night before.

"RATS! Really big ones."

Then they pitched in and began cleaning up the dining room while their host shuffled up and down in his wooden clodhoppers, cursing each time he stepped on a broken fortune cookie or a discarded piece of shrimp. "The fucking pigs," he murmured as he dragged a bucket of soapy water across the floor and began scrubbing down some chairs.

Finding himself alone with Betty gave Probo the chance he'd been waiting for to speak to her without the twins around. He was having second thoughts about their conversation of the night before, and he wanted to set a few things straight. "You know," he began somewhat timorously, trying to avoid the woman's deep, hypnotic eyes. "You've had quite a bit to say about the twins and their music, and I understand that...after all, you are their manager. But I'm not sure you understand where *I'm* coming from. As I told you yesterday, I'm here in Chicago trying to make a name for myself, not to provide backup for a couple of Alice Cooper wannabes who seem incapable of pronouncing more than a half dozen words between them. I need to return home with my head held high, not between my legs as some folks would like to see. After all the humiliation I've been through I don't intend to play second fiddle to anyone, ever again." As Probo unleashed this half-hearted show of bravado, he waited expectantly for Betty to summon the shaggy-headed carnivores from the next room to come in and pick over whatever choice portions of his hide appealed to them. But much to his surprise she simply smiled that warm, irresistible smile of hers that made the soft, chewy caramel at the center of his being run like molasses on a hot tin plate. "Oh, was it really that bad?" she cooed in a voice so tender and inviting that the diminutive elephant wanted to snuggle right up between her legs, the way he did with his mother, the famous Molly, when he was just a toddler. But that wouldn't improve his situation much. Here he was, in an unfamiliar place with no one to relate to but a couple of moronic nineteen-year-olds, a half-witted drummer and a former carny with a suspicious past. For the first time since leaving home Probo began to reflect on all that had happened to him. Much of it was just a blur…months of loneliness and despair as he made his way from one town to another, wondering what sort of future lay ahead of him. But before his emotions could give way to tears, Probo heard a musical, bird-like voice fluttering at his ears like a pair of wings.

"Fear not, young friend," said the enchantress affectionately. "You will find your way home. And before you do, you will discover that we're all in this together…you, me, Opie, even the twins. Like you, we live in a world where everything of any real value has been trivialized beyond recognition - even language itself. The fact is, Probo, the rabbit-hole down which we've been led is made up of *words,* not images. Sometimes the only way to deal with all this absurdity is to counter it with some absurdities of your own, and by so doing once again become master of your own voice."

"But who is behind these words of which you speak?" asked the elephant as he was drawn deeper and deeper into the woman's emerald-green eyes.

"Why, the jackdaws and jabbernowls that inhabit the airwaves, that's who," she answered. "The carnival barkers and sideshow frauds lurking behind the screen, preaching to the rest of us about hope and sacrifice while they count their millions. They are the political pundits and media clowns who turn every disaster into a spectacle while dangling half-baked ideas and gratuitous sex before the masses like bright, shiny ornaments on Christmas Eve. The truth is, Probo, if you don't live by your own illusions, you'll live by somebody else's. That is the only reality."

"Gee, I never thought about that," Probo said wistfully, wondering if some of that gratuitous sex might be waiting for him under *his* tree that holiday season. He was beginning to feel more at ease around this strange and wonderful woman. She must have been quite a beauty in her younger days, he reflected. Wasn't too bad now, either, he thought as she threw him a suggestive wink that made the soft, chewy caramel at the center of his being turn hard as saltwater taffy on a cold December night. As the conversation continued, Probo confided in Betty about events back home and the despicable plot to have his name left off the circus posters. He told her, too, about the ill-fated accident involving his mother and about the betrayal of his fellow band members, news of which had reached him only the day before. Betty, in turn, talked about her years working the amusement circuit and traveling from town to town with little Opie in tow. Before long they were laughing and chatting away like a couple of old friends. Feeling a bit overconfident perhaps, the ever-curious elephant made a veiled attempt to inquire into some of the stories Opie had told him about his grandmother. "So, uh...tell me," he ventured cautiously, "what did folks like you do to keep yourselves busy after the carnival closed down at night? Those small towns don't offer much in the way of entertainment, do they?" Betty was too quick to miss his meaning.

"Oh...*that*," she intoned dryly, throwing the mule-faced drummer in the adjacent room a disgruntled look through the open doorway. Her eyes locked on him like the horns of a bull. Probo could almost smell the blood.

"No problem," Betty laughed spiritedly, brushing the grey locks from her face and drawing a cigarette from her purse. "That was some years ago. I was a lot slimmer then and could still turn a few heads. It started one night, just outside Collinsville, when a group of farm boys came around after closing time looking to hook up with some of the girls that traveled with the show. Well, I liked a party as much as anyone in those days, so a bunch of us ended up getting high and riding around half-naked on the carousel. Nothing serious mind you...just some silly, good-natured fun. I pulled out this old riding crop I just happened to have and began lashing away at the merry-go-round horses, yelling *'Whoop, whoop, giddy-up there'* as those bare-assed farm boys reeled and rocked like a bunch of drunken cowboys. Well, a few days later, just after we pulled into the next town, there was another group of men hanging around. They had heard about our little escapade and wanted some of the same. In fact, we encountered the same thing at every town we came to, and before long it got to be a real problem. That's when I decided we needed to do something to discourage these troublemakers."

Probo's eyes grew wide as saucers as Betty knocked an ash from her cigarette and crossed her shapely legs. He could still hear Wang in the next room stomping around in his wooden booties, swirling the mop and cursing at every misplaced won ton on his newly tiled floor. *"Rats...really big ones,"* he repeated over and over as if it were some sort of mantra. In his mind's eye Probo envisioned a bearded, two-hundred-pound Little Dutch Boy who had gone berserk. One thing he could say about the medication he was on...it didn't much help his condition, but the things he saw when he closed his eyes were sure worth the price of admission.

"We had this fellow who traveled with the carnival," Betty explained as Probo listened attentively. "A tall, weird-looking guy who dressed up like a clown, passing out candy, balloons and such to the children. Together, he and I came up with this plan where the next time a bunch of these yahoos came around looking to party I'd slip into a sexy pair of jeans and lure them onto the carousel - which, from the stories they'd heard was exactly what they expected. Then I'd playfully suggest that we all drop our britches and climb up in the saddle for a little romp. Once they were strapped in good and tight, I'd start the ride up as fast as it would go. Just when they looked like they were about to barf up their grits my accomplice would leap onto the spinning platform and gather up their trousers - the idea being to send them home without them. That was the plan. Instead, the stupid bastard got carried away, slipped up behind these fellows and started smacking away at their randy asses with some item or other from his clown's bag of tricks. All the while he'd be throwing kisses at them and shouting, 'Hey there, sweet cheeks...why don't you climb down off that big, bucking mount of yours and give Floppy here a ride?' Needless to say, not one of those fellows ever returned."

"Wow, that's incredible!" Probo cried out ecstatically, his face glowing with excitement. "And I take it that once word leaked out about the incident, you stopped having guys hanging around the carnival at night." Betty glanced down at her cigarette, studied the long, grey ash dangling from the tip, and with a slight look of regret responded, "Well, not exactly. Apparently, news about what happened never did get out. Needless to say, those who had heard about events back in Collinsville continued coming around."

"I don't get it," said Probo, visibly agitated. "I mean, what could have gone wrong?" Betty took a long drag on her cigarette, held it in for a moment…then, with a toss of her head, let it out slowly. "Well, let me ask you this…," she remarked as the elephant waited expectantly, held captive in the gaze of her eyes. "Would *you* tell anyone you've just had your ass whipped with a rubber chicken by some bozo wearing nothing but a jockstrap and a big, rubber nose? I don't think so. Keep in mind…these boys went home changed men, Probo. *Changed men."*

Probo didn't perform well during the group's first rehearsal later that afternoon. He told the others he was out of practice, not having touched his instrument in several weeks. Truth was, he had a queasy feeling in the pit of his stomach. Maybe it was nerves. Maybe it was a side effect from all the medication he'd been taking. More likely than not it was just the weirdness of it all, what with the one-eyed children of the dead howling at his back like a couple of banshees and the mule-faced drummer beating at his snare as if he were trying to make a nickel fall out. But after an hour or two things began to settle into place. Much to his surprise, Probo discovered that the twins' mournful, dirge-like vocals had a strange, inventive quality to them which inspired him to come up with some interesting improvisations of his own. Opie, too, had mellowed out a bit and was providing some tasteful accompaniment on the drums. As the day's practice drew to a close, it occurred to Probo that the twins' much-heralded ability to cast a spell over their audiences hadn't materialized - at least insofar as he was concerned. Laughing quietly to himself, he scoffed, "More of Opie's bullshit. He must think I'm some kind of idiot." Probo glanced over to where the Wisconsin kid sat crouched behind his drums like a mechanical monkey waiting for a coin to fall through the slot. The monkey simply grinned and looked away.

Following a quiet evening and a good night's rest, Probo awoke early Friday morning, eager to continue rehearsing and preparing for the following night's performance. He was encouraged by the group's progress and was equally impressed with Betty's knowledge of music and the helpful suggestions she offered now and then. She, in turn, seemed especially taken with the elephant, and she urged the talented trumpet player to show off his versatility by playing lead on some old love songs from the '30s and '40s that everyone was familiar with. In fact, she was rather adamant about it - arguing that the group needed to reach out to people in the audience who might not be all that receptive to the more jazz-influenced pieces the group had been working on. Everyone seemed pleased...except, as usual, the curiously garbed Gornisht twins in their death-metal attire with moods to match. These two rarely expressed any emotion other than the insolent scorn typical of their generation. It was apparent that moaning was all they *could* do, even when they spoke...which wasn't often.

Most of what poured from their brooding lips was a sort of plaintive cry reminiscent of beached whales calling out to one another, or some Beverly Hills housewife whining about the paint job on the ceiling while her equally disinterested husband rides her like a jockey with his eye on another horse's ass.

Later that day, as the afternoon practice drew to a close, Probo thought he noticed something odd about one of the twins - not that everything about these two characters wasn't odd to begin with. At first he couldn't quite put his finger on it, but slowly it dawned on him. One of the pair had a prominent, well-healed scar just above his exposed eye. From all appearances it had been there for some time. Was it possible he hadn't noticed it before, Probo asked himself? Hardly, and yet what was the likelihood that one - or even both of the moribund youths - had placed the leather patches they always wore over the 'wrong' eye upon awakening that morning? "No, that's ridiculous," Probo murmured as he stuffed his horn into his worn-out suitcase. "Still," he reflected, "there's something fishy going on here, but I can't tell what it is." So the hungry elephant shrugged it off as a mood of the moment and headed for the kitchen to see what the restaurant's busy owner was cooking up for dinner. One thing was certain though, Probo told himself. If this new band of theirs didn't bring in a shit-load of customers come Saturday night...he was history.

8. A Toke for Jesus

Saturday morning Probo and the rest of the group put in one last rehearsal. The arrangements were sounding pretty tight by then, due in part to Betty's keen ear and insightful direction. It was obvious why the twins had chosen her to be their manager. Probo wondered where she had developed her appreciation of music, especially her love of the trumpet. Wang had alluded to Betty's having a thing for horn players, but given the look that passed between them that first day Probo thought it best not to inquire as to what that 'thing' was. Meanwhile, he was soaring to new heights on his instrument, delivering sharp, sonorous tones that made the fine glassware tucked away in Wang's cupboards resonate with a high-pitched ringing of their own. Even the anteater, whose shrill arpeggios made young women shiver and old women strut like roosters, couldn't have matched the high C's that pierced the air each time Probo raised his trumpet to his lips. The band was showing a good deal of promise, and Probo hoped that everything would turn out for the best after all. Still, there was a part of him that missed the sad-eyed simian and the one-legged anteater with the impeccably groomed snout. These Gornisht twins were nowhere near the musicians Mumps and Shakey were, and Probo missed his old friends' camaraderie more than he realized.

It was just before noon when Probo realized that something was wrong. His eyes were red and swollen…his lips, dry and chapped…and his head felt like a ten-cent balloon blown up to the size of a dirigible. He could still play his horn, but it caused him a fair amount of discomfort. "Poor thing," said Betty, throwing her arms around the undersized elephant as if he were a big, stuffed doll. In fact, it was precisely *because* of his size that people had such affection for the cuddly-looking trumpet player. Unfortunately, when you're a young male trying to impress the ladies it's a bit unnerving to constantly hear, "Oh, look mommy…isn't he cute? He's so *tiny*!" No wonder Probo loved to parade on stage with that big, shiny horn of his. When you're *tiny*, blowing the kazoo just don't cut it.

"Poor thing," cooed the green-eyed carny as she led Probo to a quiet corner of the room. "You must be having a reaction to the MSG in all that fancy cooking Wang's been dishing up for you. I told you to go easy on that stuff, but you just wouldn't listen."

"So you did," Probo said wearily. "But how could I resist those heaping portions of 'Pimp Satay with Lice and Peanut Sauce?' You know how I love peanuts. And how could I say no to the succulent 'Peking Dick' that Wang kept pushing at me? It's the specialty of the house, you know." Betty smiled quietly to herself and gave the circus lad another squeeze, the way his mother did just before she admonished her teary three-year-old to always say his prayers, then slipped off in search of the great elephant burial ground where she hoped to lay her tired bones down among those of her ancestors. As fate would have it, the site had been cleared to make way for a new shopping mall with a string of fast food joints. Where she ended up, no one knows for sure.

Betty reached into her handbag and pulled out a small mirror she carried. Studying her face carefully while she fixed her makeup, she consoled the elephant with some motherly advice of her own. "The way you're feeling," she said, "I don't think it wise for you to push yourself too hard this evening. I know this is your big night and all, but you need to give that lip a rest. Maybe we should shorten the set by dropping those old love songs I asked you to learn, or...say, I have an idea! What if we could find someone to *sing* them? That way, instead of playing lead, you could simply fill in on accompaniment and save your strength for the rest of the show. Of course, it's only a suggestion," Betty added, pouring those big, green eyes of hers down on Probo like August moons. "I don't know," said the distressed trumpet player, looking a bit greenish himself. "Where will we find someone to sing at this late hour? Say, you have a pretty nice voice...maybe you could sing them."

"Me? No, don't be silly," Betty said laughingly as she primped her hair and applied a fresh coat of lipstick. "Let me think. You know...Wang used to sing a bit. Nothing spectacular, mind you, but he can carry a tune. He might do it. He's very shy though. It will take some convincing. Let me talk to him."

"But won't he be busy in the kitchen?" asked Probo, swooning on his feet. Betty dropped the mirror back into her purse, pulled out a fresh pack of Luckies and began to tear it open.

"Not a problem," she answered. "Even as we speak Wang and the others are hard at work preparing tonight's meal. Once the guests are seated, the food will be brought out and everyone will be served at once. That will allow Wang to join the rest of the group on stage once the performance begins."

"Well, I guess that will work," groaned the elephant, too sick to think much more on the matter. "Excellent," said Betty with a sigh of relief. "Don't worry about a thing, Probo. This will still be your night. My advice now is for you to drink plenty of water, flush that MSG out of your system and get some rest. Chances are you'll be feeling better by dinner time."

"You're always telling me not to worry," said Probo, showing his irritation. "To tell you the truth, that's what makes me worry."

Probo slept fitfully the next few hours, going over in his mind what Betty had told him about the evening's plans. According to her there would be a one-time seating around seven o'clock. The event was being widely promoted as A Night to Remember. Probo had never actually seen the posters and other materials Betty had talked about designing - the explanation being that time was running short, so she handled everything by phone: placing ads in the newspapers, contacting radio stations, notifying the twins' friends and followers back in Wisconsin about the goings-on down in Chicago. At least that's what Probo was told when he inquired into the matter. "Don't worry," Betty assured him. "By the time the doors open, even the folks in Peanutville will have heard about you. Believe me, there's going to be a huge turnout for this event. Standing room only…for those who can stand, of course." Probo was a bit dubious, but there was little he could do.

By the time Probo dragged himself up off the floor of the back room it was nearly six o'clock. Still feeling somewhat woozy he grabbed his belongings, wound his way past the busy crew working in the kitchen and headed for the alley behind the restaurant for a bit of air. He also wanted a smoke. Pulling his horn from his suitcase, he leaned up against the side of the building and watched the sun, orange and bloated like a big balloon, sink beneath the rooftops amidst the evening haze. The days were getting longer, he noticed - always a sure indication that the new circus season was underway. By now posters would be up all over circus town announcing the Peanutville Days parade to be held the first weekend in July. Somewhere at the top would be the circus master's name spelled out in big, bold letters followed by that of the various band members, the clowns and acrobats, the guest performers and the dignitaries who would march in the procession. Shedding a tear Probo raised the trumpet to his dry, chapped lips, flinched at the pain and began a slow, melodious lament which spelled out in dark, somber tones just how homesick he really felt. Perhaps he was the one exception to Betty's assertion that no one ever sang his own sad song. Setting the instrument to one side, he fumbled in his pocket for the small pouch he'd placed there moments before. It wasn't as full as it used to be. Not to worry, he thought. The medicine wasn't doing him much good anyway. A few more weeks and it would all be gone. If his condition wasn't cleared up by then he might as well take his big, sorry ass down to the river and throw it in. Regardless of how the band performed that night, his chances of achieving the recognition he was longing for were slim. The people of Chicago might take warmly to him, but would they throw peanuts and chant his name the way folks in Peanutville did once upon a time?

Moments later Probo was back on his horn wailing out some of those old circus tunes he so loved to play. As he worked his way through the opening lines of his all-time favorite, the *Baby Elephant Walk,* it began to dawn on him that what really mattered was not the wounded pride he'd been nursing ever since leaving home…but the music itself. "My God," he exclaimed, stunned by this unexpected revelation. "It's not about *me,"* he stammered, "it's about the music and the sheer joy of playing it." It was a momentous discovery for someone accustomed to having been at the center of attention most of his life. Even after the unfortunate incident that forced his mother into retirement, Probo continued to be the darling of the circus world, trading in his trusty kazoo for the big, shiny instrument everyone now knew him for. For years people talked about him, whispering, "There he goes…Molly's son, heir to the throne of Peanutville." Not the sort of adulation anyone would give up willingly. As Probo reflected more on the matter, he also began to realize that the anteater wasn't really to blame for the fateful accident that took his leg, thus leading to the flood of sympathy that enabled him to steal the spotlight from the celebrated trumpet player. Sure, the anteater had no business snooping around the bear cage…but then, the one-eyed Mongolian with the gold tooth who sold the bear to the circus swore that it was gentle as a lamb. Or maybe he said something else…after all, his English was pretty garbled. Perhaps they should have taken a clue from the local farmer who'd reported finding some of his livestock mangled and half-eaten out in the fields about that time.

Probo reached over to a nearby window ledge and picked up the freshly rolled joint he'd set there moments before. Most people don't know that elephants are huge ganja users...smoke nothing but the best, and with good reason. Nearly all of these noble but timid creatures suffer from poor eyesight, so much so that many of them have placed their hopes in medical research showing the active ingredient in cannabis, THC, to be of benefit to those with certain eye disorders. Unfortunately, even the regular doses Probo was taking did little to improve his vision, despite assurances from some of his hip, young elephant friends that he would see noticeable results within in a few short months. It was they who had encouraged the nearsighted lad to spend his hard-earned savings on a sizable supply of the sweet-smelling herb...which Madame Zuzu, the circus' self-proclaimed apothecary, was happy to provide after jotting down a prescription on the back of a horoscope.

As Probo reflected on these matters, a disheveled and unkempt man in an ill-fitting overcoat and mismatched socks slipped unnoticed from behind a nearby dumpster where he had been drowning his troubles in a brown paper bag. For an instant the two of them stood there in the fading light like figures in a surrealist painting: the elephant, his reflection distorted in a nearby window...the stranger staring blindly past him with cataract-covered eyes. The man listened intently as Probo once more tried to squeeze all the pain and anguish of his suffering heart through the narrow bell of his instrument. Tossing the empty bottle aside, the man staggered over, feeling his way along the wall of the building until he got to within a few feet of the celestial sound Jutting his bristled chin skyward, he sniffed at the air and muttered in a coarse, foul breath, "Hey man, can you spare a smoke?" The startled musician lowered his horn and stared silently at the intruder. Despite his appearance the man had a certain demeanor about him that suggested he had once been a person of means, with a wife and children perhaps, and a successful career. "Sure," said Probo somewhat apprehensively as he reached over and placed the smoldering spliff between the man's cracked and dirty fingers. The stranger drew deeply, holding it in like a condemned prisoner enjoying his last cigarette. "Roll your own, eh?" he remarked, exhaling with a dazed and euphoric look. "That's the best. Those packaged jobs are full of cancer. *Real* tobacco…that's what I like."

"Keep it," said Probo, returning the mouthpiece to his lips. His curious companion again drew from the slow-burning roach while sad, discordant notes poured from the trumpet player's lips and lingered in the night air like the fumes emanating from the blind man's mouth. Probo's thoughts drifted back to his childhood and the cheering crowds with their screams of horror and delight each time Adolf, the one-handed lion tamer, drew his mangled stub from the creature's mouth and held it out in one of his stiff-armed salutes for everyone to see. Even the toothless old beast got off on the joke and received a tasty reward for its efforts. Some years later one of the younger animals thrilled the audience by giving the jackbooted trainer with the hated whip and funny little moustache a nice bloody stub to match the first.

"Roll your own, eh? That's what I like."

"Play that horn for me, Gabriel!" the man with the ragged coat and unkempt hair blurted out suddenly, tears welling in his glazed and empty eyes. "Play that horn for me, angel...play *Coming Home to Jesus*." Probo stood dumbfounded as the high grade Columbian he'd inhaled a few minutes before ran rampant through his brain. In the distance he could hear the sounds of people arriving at the restaurant. A quick glance at his watch told him it was nearly seven. Panic struck the circus lad as the man drew closer and began breathing in his ear. "I've been walking these streets for thirteen years...," he gasped, his sightless eyes glistening like opals in the setting sun. "Thirteen years, warning everyone I meet that the Day of Judgment is at hand. And now, thank you Jesus, it has finally arrived...in a blaze of glory with trumpets blaring, just as I foretold."

"Hold on there," Probo sputtered, struggling to make sense of the man's ravings as his bewhiskered face, glowing with rapture, rose up like a demented genie's from a cloud of purple smoke. All at once he lunged at the elephant, grabbed hold of his jacket and cried out in a frantic, excited voice, "Jesus...sweet Jesus! I can see. I CAN SEE! It's a miracle. Thank you, Jesus, thank you!"

"No, no...hold on there," Probo demanded as the man began running his weather-beaten hands over the musician's head and shoulders, crying out for all the world to hear, "Bless you, bless you Jesus...I can see!" Probo could feel the man's whiskey-laden breath mingling with his own and the perfumed horror of an abscessed tooth reaching out from its dark, dank cavern. The beleaguered trumpet player was about to give up his Chicken

Chow Fun from the night before, when all at once the man began stammering and speaking in tongues. "Wuh, wuh, wuh, wuh, wuh. Wuh, wuh, wuh, wuh…wait a minute! Wuh, wuh, wuh…WHAT THE FUCK? You ain't Jesus. An elephant? A fuh, fuh, fuh…**FUCKING ELEPHANT?**" A fresh burst of saliva hit Probo in the eye with each subsequent 'fuh'.

"Oh shit," Probo murmured, tearing himself free of the man's grip and stumbling backward in a desperate bid for the safety of Wang's kitchen. Reaching the door he clambered inside, slamming it tightly behind him and locking it. "Whew!" he exclaimed breathlessly as Wang looked on in his ten-dollar hairpiece and wooden shoes. "This sure isn't Peanutville."

"It ain't Holland, either," the cook remarked caustically, wiping his hands on a towel and kicking some bean curd from his foot. "*The fucking pigs.*"

9. May His Eye Rot in Hell

Things were going crazy now. People were pouring into the restaurant...elderly people with canes and walkers, some in wheelchairs, others too feeble to walk without the help of a dozen or so scruffy-looking men in matching tan jackets with the words *Vote Democratic* stenciled on the back. Probo watched from the back room as one of these Good Samaritans led a man with dark glasses and a walking stick to his seat. "That's it, George...right there. Okay, stop. Now you can sit down." The man with the dark glasses felt around the table with his thin, frail hands as if searching for something. "Are we voting today?" he asked. "They told me we're voting today. You know I never miss an election."

"Not today, George," the Good Samaritan responded, throwing one of his tan-clad buddies a sarcastic smile. "November, this November. Then you can vote as often as you like...if you're still around, that is. If not, we'll see that someone votes for you."

Pushing and shoving their way in behind the crowd were several men in wrinkled sharkskin suits that looked as if they had been slept in. Each wore a little sticker pasted to his lapel that read *'Hi. My name is...'* followed by some indecipherable scrawl.

Two of the men had cameras slung across their backs, while all of them clutched open pints of whiskey or cans of beer from which they took long swigs every now and then. Like the sick and elderly before them, not one of them could walk a straight line.

Betty stood at the door greeting visitors and shaking hands. She was dressed in some bizarre getup she had fashioned out of leather and lace - half Marquis de Sade, half Swan Lake. The only thing missing was a bear on a chain and she would have fit right in with the Russian Circus. Standing alongside her and whispering in her ear was her cousin Zyg. Probo recognized him at once as the man from the hotel. He was directing traffic and barking orders to the men in the tan jackets. As the room filled to capacity and the last guest - a confused-looking gentleman with a protective helmet wrapped around his head - was seated, a final group of visitors arrived. They were richly attired in expensive suits, each sporting a large ring on his finger, one of which was the size of the mole on the precinct captain's neck. They were escorted by an entourage of sniveling lackeys who greeted Betty's cousin warmly and accompanied him to the front of the chamber where the low, flimsily constructed platform would serve as a dais.

The tables had been arranged in long rows, end to end, cafeteria style. People were crammed in together like prisoners in a mess hall, their canes and walkers stacked up between them like bars of a cage. Most of these retirement home inmates were grey and balding, hunched over or nearly blind. Watching the commotion from the back room, Probo wondered what it all meant. Where were the groupies he had been told about? Where were the pretty, young college girls who were supposed to drive down from Wisconsin to see the twins perform and cheer the band on with cries of "Move that pigskin" and "One more for the Gipper"?

"Better get it together, son," Opie teased the elephant as he slipped up behind him, peering through the open doorway into the chamber beyond. "It won't be long now. A few more speeches and then we're on. Talk about a captive audience, eh?" Probo turned beet-red. "What are you talking about? Where are the groupies you promised? Where are all the young fans the Gornisht Brothers were supposed to attract? These people don't look like jazz lovers to me. In fact, some of them look like they were born before jazz was invented."

"Overflow crowd," Opie said matter-of-factly. "Not much we can do about it. We had to turn away six or seven gorgeous babes who drove all the way in from Milwaukee. We told them to come back tomorrow and we'd offer them a free brunch and the chance to meet you."

"Really?" said Probo, his blood racing at the thought of all that hot, young Republican booty. "They want to meet *me*?" Smiling softly to himself, the drummer replied, "You bet. In fact, if I were a betting man I'd say there are a few gals here tonight with your name written across their heart. Better watch your step, Casanova." Probo squinted hard in an effort to make out the bent and shrunken figures lined up behind the tables like mummies in a crypt. His mind turned to slush at the thought that there might be some groupies among them after all...and they were all gunning for him. "What's that Zyg fellow doing here?" Probo snapped as yet another wave of paranoia swept over him. "And what's with the cameras?"

"There's a convention in town, dummy," Opie answered with an air of indignation. "Television reporters and news journalists from all over the state. Some of them are staying at Zyg's place. He brought them over to catch the performance. There's a good chance you and I will be on the front page by morning, my friend, so get it together. Say…you don't look so well. All that MSG you've been eating still got you down? You really ought to lay off that stuff."

"I haven't been eating MSG," Probo retorted. "It was in the food that…oh, forget it. I'll be okay and ready to perform."

"Hurry up, there," Wang shouted as the twins rushed to and fro inside the kitchen gathering up steaming trays and platters to be carried out to the restless crowd. A moment later Betty entered the back room taking bites from a flat, doughy object she carried in her hand. It didn't look to Probo like anything he had ever seen before. Feeling his appetite starting to return he asked what it was. "It's a blintze," Betty said cheerfully. "Want a taste?"

"A blintze? And what about those other things?" the elephant inquired, taking note of the heavy trays making their way into the dining room. Betty stepped over to where the two circus buddies stood peering through the doorway. "Well, let's take a look. I see some lox and bagels, some gefilte fish, some delicious kishke, plenty of matzo ball soup…but don't worry, Probo. They probably don't have any MSG in them."

"I don't care about the MSG," barked the elephant as the freckle-faced kid looked on smartly. "I'm just trying to understand. Gefilte fish, matzo ball soup, lox and bagels…those are what, Jewish dishes?"

"What's to understand?" said the woman in the severe-looking gown with the blintze in her hand. "Wang is Jewish. So are a lot of the people here this evening. So he decided to cook up something special. Wait till you try the knishes, they're fantastic!" Probo shook his head in disbelief. "Knishes? Jewish? I thought you said Wang was an Okie…from Muskogee, you said."

"So? You think they don't have Jews in Oklahoma? Plenty of them…tough sons of bitches, too. They walk around wearing these big, black Fedoras and long, dark coats that make them look a bit like Wyatt Earp. And they're all packing huge, long-barreled Smith and Wessons that they keep tucked inside their pants…big suckers, sawed off at the end."

"Yes, but they don't shoot on Shabbas," interjected the drummer, showing off his first-hand knowledge of the Chosen People of the Sooner State.

"Opie, please…I'll do the talking. As I was saying, in parts of Oklahoma these Muskogee Jews are known as '*Muskogevites*'. Some have even taken it for their last name."

"Grandma, tell Probo about the famous actor, 'Dirty Harry' Muskogevitz," the Wisconsin lad cut in. "I love that scene where he walks into a diner on the eve of Rosh Hashanah and

94

comes upon this robber in the middle of a holdup. The two men just stand there, staring at one another, each wondering if the other will reach for his gun...when Harry gets a big grin on his face and says to the guy, 'Go ahead...*make my Yontif*.' "

"I said, that's enough already..."

"And tell Probo about the delicious grape wine they drink on the holidays. Man, that stuff will blow your ass out of the water. They even give it to their kids. Those are my kind of people. I can see why they've been chosen."

"Shhh," the youth's grandmother cautioned. "The senator is about to speak."

"...And did you know that Oklahoma is the birthplace of Clarence Nash, the guy who does Donald Duck's voice? I like Donald Duck."

"I said shut the fuck up, Opie."

Probo was still reeling from his encounter with the man in the alley. The experience had left him feeling strangely disoriented, almost as if he were a character in some really bad novel or an actor in one of those cheap propaganda films warning teenagers about the dangers of drug abuse. The paranoia was out of its cage now and raging inside him, strutting up and down the boulevards of his discombobulated brain like the high-stepping gals in the Peanutville Days parade, blowing their whistles and twirling their batons. Probo was certain that any moment the crazy

*"You think they don't have Jews in Oklahoma?
Plenty of them. Tough sons of bitches, too!"*

Muskogevite with the wooden shoes would come running out from the kitchen waving his big, sawed-off Smith and Wesson at anyone who dropped a crumb on his shiny, clean floor.

"Hey, good buddy," the drummer called out. "Snap out of it. This is no time for daydreaming. We'll be going on in a few minutes." Probo swung around to find Opie and his grandmother staring at him and whispering to one another as if he were some sort of alien that had dropped in from the sky. This of course only served to increase Probo's paranoia even more. Strange visions, fueled by the heavy doses of cannabis and MSG, turned his brain into a carnival of lights. Seconds later the room began to spin as he saw himself chained to a huge Ferris wheel that had fallen off its axle and was rolling downhill, headed straight for the dark, shark-infested waters of Lake Michigan. There was some tall, gangly lunatic chasing after it, wearing nothing but an athletic supporter and screaming something about 'wanting his chicken back'. "Sorry," came the deep, stentorian voice booming down from heaven like a clap of thunder. "We needed it for the matzo ball soup. You should try some…it's delicious!" Seconds later another voice, no less omnipotent than the first, caught Probo's attention and brought him to his senses.

"Friends, friends…thank you all for being here today. As you know, I am running for re-election as your state senator this November, and I'm counting on your support. Let me tell you a bit about my record….I am the one who introduced the bill to make the stalking of any female over the age of seventy a Class X felony. We don't need all those perverts out there snatching purses and copping a feel from helpless women who can't defend themselves. None of you gentlemen are safe either, from what I've heard. With your help, I'll return to Springfield this fall and amend the bill to include persons of *all* genders. My God, what is our society coming to? Blame it on these foreigners, I always say. Well, not to worry with your friend Paddy McGrafft at the helm....but you can call me *Pat*."

"Isn't he wonderful?" said one white-haired octogenarian to her lady friend as the room filled with applause. "Say," she added, adjusting the hem of her pink gingham dress. "Didn't we see him in Las Vegas some years ago?" Her friend reflected for a moment, then answered. "No, I think it was last week outside the supermarket. He was shaking hands and passing out campaign literature. But you're right...he does have that Las Vegas look about him."

"And so friends, remember to vote for yours truly come November. And now, it's my pleasure to introduce a fine young man running for President of the Water Reclamation District...Seymour Backslapper. I knew his father, Winky Backslapper, who served as an appellate judge for many years. And let me say that in times like these, with water bills skyrocketing and the cost of flushing the toilet or taking a bath out of many peoples' reach...you don't need someone who will piss your tax dollars down the drain like those bastards in Washington. And now, let's all put our hands together for *the next president of the...*"

Probo looked on as Zyg's men shuffled from table to table giving a sharp nudge to anyone who appeared to be nodding or not paying enough attention. Moments later the speaker stepped down from the stage and headed for the sidelines where he began posing for the cameras. Probo didn't much care for politicians. They didn't have real jobs like most people. They couldn't juggle, except maybe the public coffers. They couldn't walk the high wire, and they couldn't ride bareback atop a galloping pony as it leaped through a burning hoop. All they were good at was riding aloft on other peoples' shoulders, which gave them the appearance of being much taller than they were. But unlike the circus midgets, who were also adept at such antics, these blow-hards preferred facing backwards - which, needless to say, was a bit hard on their supporters. The reason for this was obvious: since most of these windbags had no idea where they were coming from, they thought it wise to keep a constant eye on where they'd *been*. Watching McGrafft prance around in front of the flashing bulbs reminded Probo of that *other* pompous clown, Hornbuckle. If only he could lay his hands on one of those big, sawed-off Smith and Wessons like the Jews had. He would shove it down the guy's throat and make him say '*ah*'.

Wang and the twins, meanwhile, were busy rushing about carrying the last of the trays and dishes out to the crowd. Most of the guests were well into their meal, while others poked around suspiciously at the chopped liver and other delicacies set before them. "Are you sure they're kosher?" asked the man with the portable breathing device as he inspected the potato latkes. "Of course they're kosher," Wang assured him, setting a pitcher down and adjusting his hairpiece. "One hundred percent kosher."

"Forget it then," said the man. "I hate kosher. Bring me a ham sandwich."

"Now, now," urged one of Zyg's tan-jacketed assistants in an effort to calm the man down. "If you don't behave yourself, I won't help you fill out your absentee ballot come November."

"You schmuck!" the man cried out accusingly, inhaling deeply from his oxygen mask. "The last time you helped me vote that thief with the glass eye got elected and my prescription costs nearly doubled. He should rot in hell."

"But Max," said a sweet old lady sitting at the man's side. "He's not dead."

"Well, then his eye should rot in hell...wherever it is."

Wang entered the back room looking harried and wiping his hands on a towel. "This is it," he said, staring nervously at his ex-wife. "I'm going to wash up and change while the twins finish in the kitchen. They've got their stage outfits on under their aprons, so they'll be ready as soon as that fellow up there is done speaking. I'll join the rest of you in a minute. By the way, Probo...have you seen the play list?" Probo demurred while Opie shoved a crumpled piece of paper in front of him. "Ah, yes," the elephant laughed weakly. "I guess it *would* help to know the order of the songs. I assume you've got the lyrics down. I'll be there to back you up...but other than that, the stage is all yours."

"Don't worry about a thing, young fellow. Those songs

are old favorites of mine. I know them well. Rest assured I'll do my best to make you all proud of me. You've got a great little band here, and I wouldn't want to do anything to embarrass you. Besides, those folks out there are waiting to hear the hot, new trumpet player everyone's been talking about. They're not here to see me. I'm only glad I can help."

Probo blushed and looked away. He felt a sudden burst of affection for the man with the wooden shoes and ridiculous hairpiece. He must have been quite dashing in his younger days, he thought. He wondered why Wang and Betty were no longer together. They certainly seemed compatible enough now, he reflected.

"Oh, one more thing Probo," Wang called out as he rushed from the room. "That third song of the set...I was wondering if the band could speed it up a bit and maybe take it to the key of C. That would work better for me. I may want to improvise a little. I guess we all have a bit of the ham in us...even kosher guys like me."

"Sure thing," laughed the trumpet player. "I'll inform the others. Oh, oh...that guy at the microphone sounds as if he's about to wrap it up. You'd better hurry."

"Good enough. I'll make my appearance right after Betty finishes the introductions. Other than that, all I can say young fellow is...break a leg."

10. The Beast Unveiled

As the last speaker stepped down from the stage, Zyg's men quickly cleared the aisles in order to allow the various state and local officials to work the room, which in the parlance of Chicago politics meant passing out campaign literature, shaking hands, kissing the ladies and smiling up close and personal to people who could only wish they could afford the dental work these guys had. When the men in their Brooks Brothers suits and large pinky rings were finished schmoozing, they left the premises as suddenly as they had arrived, taking their sniveling lackeys with them. Only McGrafft and his greasy-looking handler stayed behind to watch the performance.

Betty entered the room first, followed by Opie, then Probo and the twins. Most of the people crammed behind the long rows of tables had already finished eating and were busy squirreling away leftovers in their coats and bags for a late-night snack. Betty gave the signal and someone dimmed the overhead lights, leaving only the paper lanterns to illuminate the premises with their eerie, red glow. Opie ascended the stage first, settling in behind his drums like a NASCAR driver sliding into the cockpit of his Formula 1. Checking the sound level, he slammed his foot against the bass drum pedal with a terrific thud. Had it been the gas pedal of his beloved Chevy at least five bystanders would already be dead. Probo took up a position to the left of the stage while the twins mounted the platform and situated themselves behind the second of two microphones just to the drummer's right. Pressing their long, black manes together they looked like something washed up from the ocean and left to die in the sand. The shark was in the house.

Primping the ruffles of her impossible-looking leather and lace outfit, Betty stepped to the front of the stage and took a long, low bow. As she did so, the hem of her hoop-shaped skirt flipped out behind her like a wind-torn umbrella. Opie, who had a front row view of the event, sat frozen at his drums, the words 'sweet potato pie' forming on his lips. Straightening up and pulling the garment down around her long, shapely legs Betty leaned into the microphone and began to speak. "I want to thank each of you for being here tonight," she intoned in that singsong voice of hers. "And thank you also for your patience while our good friends from state and local government delivered their important messages. And now, it's time to move on to what you all have been waiting for. We are honored to present to you one of the most exciting new musical groups ever to grace the Chicago scene. We have with us tonight a fabulous young trumpet player, direct from the circus capital of the world...Peanutville, Indiana. And on the drums, straight from the homophobic capital of the world - Madapahadawanee, Wisconsin - the one and only *Opie*! Last but not least are a couple of young singers, twins in fact, whose unique style of emoting is unlike anything you've heard before - or gauging from the age of most of you, ever will again. They will be providing backup accompaniment for our guest vocalist, the man you have to thank for the outstanding meal you enjoyed this evening. And so, without further ado I present to you the incomparable...*Wang and the Gornisht twins...featuring Probo the bull elephant on trumpet.*"

A round of applause rose up indifferently from the sated, overfed audience, most of whom leaned back in their seats poking at leftovers or picking their teeth. One elderly gentleman, thinking no one would notice, pulled a full set of dentures from his mouth and set them on the table. Another man, struggling with a bagel, stared at them enviously. Before the evening was out they would disappear.

Without further fanfare a tall, well-dressed man, clean-shaven with a full head of impeccably groomed hair entered the room. He nodded bashfully to the crowd as he made his way onto the makeshift stage. The woman in the hoop skirt handed him the microphone, stepped down and with some difficulty settled into her seat. Despite his shyness the man had the look of someone who was no stranger to this sort of thing: cool and confident, even a bit haughty perhaps. Probo scarcely recognized Wang in his svelte, double-breasted jacket with the white carnation pinned to the lapel. Only the wooden shoes protruding from the cuffs of his neatly tailored pants gave him away. Standing patiently with his face to the audience, he waited for Opie and the twins to begin the slow, mournful introduction to the familiar tear-jerker, *Forget Me Not, My Love*. Moments later Probo joined in on the trumpet, following the restaurant owner's lead as the unlikely crooner took control of the song, wending his way through the more difficult passages as only an accomplished performer might do.

Leaning forward and staring seductively into the eyes of several women at a nearby table, the man at the microphone murmured those immortal words: *'Though our paths may part, deep in your heart...forget me not, my love.'* Corny stuff, but the crowd ate it up.

Despite some discomfort Probo pressed his lips tightly to the mouthpiece, releasing a clear, resplendent accompaniment that beautifully embellished the singer's exquisite phrasing. The twins too proved themselves more than capable with their mournful complaints, while Opie dragged the brushes lazily across the snare, grinning stupidly and staring off into the distance as if his mind were out there waiting for him. As the last lines of the song... *'Your arms, your love, this lasting embrace'*...floated across the room, several ladies adrift on a dream fell into a swoon. Then came the applause...stronger this time, more enthusiastic as the dear souls dreamt of yesterday and first loves and the lost innocence of youth. Probo couldn't help but recall Betty's account about how the twins got their start, singing at funerals and such. Perhaps that's what made this night's performance all the more endearing to folks who were themselves not that far from the grave. The twins' dark, brooding harmonies blended perfectly with Wang's lively, more upbeat delivery, sounding almost as if they had performed together somewhere before...although that seemed highly improbable. Probo, too, was setting the room on fire as each note from his golden horn wrapped itself around Wang's deep, rich voice like a sylph slipping from a silken cord.

Once again, the man at the microphone held the audience spellbound as he led the band through the opening bars of that

old chestnut, *Nights like These, the Moon, and a Woman like You.*
The ladies' eyes lit up like fireflies. Those who had their
doddering husbands at their sides hung close to their lifelong
partners, steeped in memories and faraway worlds of their own.
"Isn't he wonderful?" beamed the white-haired lady in the pink
gingham dress. "Didn't we see him in Vegas some years ago?"

"Not Vegas…but somewhere," her friend said pensively,
trying to remember.

The man with the wooden shoes was in his element now,
strutting up and down the stage and making weird clip-clop sounds
that reminded Probo of the time Harry the Happy Gelding got
drunk and danced the night away on the burning porch of the
veterinarian who had relieved the former stud-horse of his most
prized possessions. The distraught animal doctor said it was a
clear case of arson; but the fire marshal from the nearby circus
declared it an accident despite evidence of kerosene-soaked girlie
magazines found under the house.

Wang, meanwhile, was in ecstasy, and he didn't care who
knew it. One might have thought the Little Dutch Boy had just had
a poke at the Little Dutch Girl out behind the windmill. Probo was
astonished at the old man's stamina. It was as if he had been
suddenly reborn or carried back to a former life of his. Even the
folks in the audience were going crazy now, caught up in the
Saturday night fever as if it were 1945 again and the war had just
ended. One dapper old fellow, dressed up in an ill-fitting veteran's
uniform, struggled to his feet and saluted the singer. Wang
returned the gesture before bending over to kiss an elderly woman

*Probo, too, was filled with admiration for the man with
the fancy new hairpiece and bedroom eyes.*

who had ambled up to the stage to slip him her phone number…and a bit of tongue besides.

If the man at the microphone had never before experienced delusions of grandeur, he certainly seemed to be enjoying them now. Even the twins, normally dour and impassive, were grinning like a couple of vultures perched above a box of newborn kittens. As the song ended and the applause died down, the Little Dutch Boy began to speak. "And now ladies and gentlemen, I'd like to say that while I was serving you earlier I happened to spot some former acquaintances of mine right here in the audience…people I haven't seen in a long, long time. Well, we're all so busy and getting older, aren't we? Ah, where have all the years gone? Those precious days of youth, those wild, crazy, passionate days of… But forgive me. I often get carried away." Pausing for a moment the sleek figure in the neatly pressed, moth-eaten suit wiped a tear from his eye and threw a longing look at his former spouse sitting a few rows from the stage. He then turned back to the audience.

"The next song is one I'm sure you'll all recognize. With your permission I'd like to dispense with the usual lyrics and offer a little something of my own as my way of saying 'thanks for the memories' to all those friends and acquaintances who have come out for this special occasion. And now…Alice, Dorothy, Mildred…this is for you. And Beatrice, there in the last row…hello darling. I see you have your husband, Sam, with you. Hellooo, Sam. I hear your prostate operation was a success. Mazel tov. You should live to be a hundred and twenty. But if not, rest assured your charming wife will be taken care of. What are friends for? And now…Maestro Probo, if you please."

Probo was grinning from ear to ear. "*Maestro Probo*," he repeated softly to himself. "He called me Maestro. Wow…this is it. This is the biggest night of my life. If only the anteater and the orangutan could see me now."

At Wang's signal the band, their spirits soaring from the wonderful reception they were receiving, sprang into the singer's third and final song of the evening. Probo was feeling a bit better and could hardly wait to get on to the rest of the set when it would be his turn to take the spotlight. For the moment, however, he too was caught up in the excitement as the man with the expensive hairpiece and bedroom eyes leaned into the microphone and whispered the words that brought thrills of anticipation to the expectant crowd:

Oh my darling,
Do you remember the night you said you
wanted my baby?
God, I was so uptight.
You asked me once…you know, I told you 'maybe'.
You asked me twice…I said, 'Your husband will know.'
You said, 'Don't worry…we won't tell him
till it shows.'

"Vhaat did he say?" asked a woman with a heavy accent, clutching her hand to her ear and turning to the man at her side. "I can't hear so goot." The man hesitated for a moment, then answered with some uncertainty, "Vell, I vouldn't know. I think

he said, *I vant you, baby, so maybe you shouldn't vorry so much.*"
The woman took a deep breath and leaned back in her chair. "Oh,
how lovely," she sighed.

Loosening his tie and unbuttoning his shirt collar, the man
with the Frank Sinatra demeanor and wooden shoes continued -
this time a bit louder:

Baby, baby...why are you staying with that guy?
I've got everything you need, and besides...I'm circumcised.
I have diamonds, I have beautiful rings,
These are just some of your favorite things.
When the rope bites, when the whip stings,
When your ass gets cold,
I like to remember that night in November
Before you got old.

Probo toyed with the valves of his trumpet, evoking bold,
brassy tones that bellowed up through the bell of his instrument
and ejaculated across the room. Opie, too, swept along by the
twins' incessant moans dragged the brushes steadily across the
snare, evoking sounds of a midnight surf breaking across the
shore. Only the twins seemed to be paying any attention to the
onslaught of darkly suggestive lyrics pouring from the
loudspeakers and the anxious murmurs washing across the room.
A wicked grin spread from one twin to the other as they gazed
through the dim light of the restaurant at the wrinkled faces staring
back in horror with eyes glazed over like those of the mid-day
catch in a Boston fish market. Once again Wang reached into his
treasure-house of memories, conjuring up images of careless youth

and reckless moments gone astray. He sang:

Baby, baby...do you remember that night
out behind the men's room? God, you were a sight!
You called your husband, told him you'd be late;
I had six Trojans...you could hardly wait.
When the rope bites, when the whip stings,
When your ass gets cold,
We'll be together, no matter the weather
Till you get old.

As the busy trumpet player finally turned his attention to the words falling from the singer's lips, the discordant notes leaping from his instrument landed on the crowd like a corpse thrown from a burning building. The twins' heartfelt moaning ground to a halt, while Opie's brushes screeched across the head of his snare like chalk on a blackboard. The room fell silent...a dead hush, deader than the tombs of Egypt. Even the man with the ecstatic expression on his face who had been fondling the small, red balls in his pocket ceased what he was doing. Another man, propped up in a wheelchair, awoke from his slumber and began to applaud. Realizing no one else was, he immediately stopped.

"Isn't he wonderful?" asked the lady in the pink gingham dress, once more turning to her friend. "Didn't we see him in Las Vegas once?"

"Oh, shut the fuck up," said the second woman, turning sharply away.

Suddenly the room exploded. "It's him!" cried someone in a thin, reedy voice from the back of the room. "It's....it's...the *meshugener*." Everyone turned to look as the frail woman rose from her seat and cried out once more, this time a bit louder, "It's...it's...the BEAST!" She then clutched her hand to her chest and collapsed face down on the table. Once again a flood of angry murmurs swept across the room. More voices were heard...men's voices this time. "It's him all right," called out one sorry-looking fellow, rage boiling in his face, "...the son of a bitch that stole my Esther from me forty years ago. He promised her a trip to Benton Harbor if she would run off with him. Imagine...Benton Harbor! My Zadie, may he rest in peace, took vacations in Benton Harbor...and that's when *he* was a boy! My God, if you're going to steal a man's wife, at least make it worth her while. Take her someplace nice...like Saugatuck for example. Saugatuck has some nice cottages, and they're reasonable."

"Fuck you, and fuck Michigan!" shouted another man, spittle flying from his mouth. "What about my Hanna? Once he was finished with her she would never let me touch her again. She hated men. Whenever she cooked my favorite blintzes they tasted like someone had wiped their ass with them. The dog wouldn't touch them. So I took them to work and gave them to my boss, Mr. Noodleman. *He* ate them."

All at once a blood-curdling scream rang out, stopping everyone in their tracks. An emaciated, red-headed woman stepped from out behind a table and pointed an accusing finger at the man on stage. "Christ!" thought Opie. "It's the 3,000-year-old mummy that served us at the diner a few nights ago...and she looks like she's all hopped up on a fresh batch of tanna leaves."

"You miserable cur," shrieked the woman as she hurled a piece of schmaltz herring at the singer. It struck his shoulder, leaving a large, greasy stain - then fell to the floor. "You sack of shit! I was to be engaged to a dentist. You hear me...A DENTIST!! My parents had it all arranged, but you... you ruined it all when you stole my honor. I mean...do you think a man like that wants a woman who opens her mouth wide on the first date?"

"But...but...but," Wang objected, stepping back from the swarm of blintzes, matzo balls and greasy chunks of sable flying at him from every direction. Opie was hunkered down behind his drum set, while the gruesome twins were clinging to one another, screaming and crying like a couple of schoolgirls. Where was the hammerhead now? Wang looked up just in time to see a salad fork hurled toward his head. Stepping back in his clumsy, oversized shoes he slipped on a piece of herring and sailed into the air, coming down heavily on the makeshift stage with a bang. "Oy, my back," he bellowed. "I think I broke something." Without a moment's hesitation the twins shot out from behind the microphone they shared and rushed to the singer's side. Bending over him, they ripped the patches from their tear-stained eyes and cried out in perfect unison, "Daddy, Daddy...are you all right?" Probo stood back and watched in total bewilderment. Despite being the largest target in the room, he seemed not to be on anyone's hit list as sliced bagels wobbling like Frisbies sailed past his head. "What the hell...?" he muttered, looking around for the band's manager. Peering through the dim light thrown off by the lanterns, he found her cowering in a corner at the back of the room. The man with the tiny, red balls was standing over her, counting on his fingers in an effort to figure how many votes he could still rely on come Election Day. McGrafft, standing a few feet away, turned to his handler and remarked, "The guy's good...really good. Maybe we can use him at my next campaign rally."

People were climbing over tables and chairs now in an attempt to get at the beleaguered singer, while others were caught up in a tangle of canes and walkers as they forced their way down the aisle with murder in their eyes. Someone grabbed hold of a nearby wheelchair and was charging the stage with it, its helpless occupant aghast at the prospect of becoming a human battering ram. A couple of women were down on their knees, crawling around like pirates with knives clenched in their teeth. The man on the breathing device was flicking a lighter at the end of the oxygen tube in hopes of turning it into a blowtorch. A few feet away a heavy-set black gentleman had forced his way to the front of the stage where he grabbed the microphone and launched into a soulful rendition of *Nobody Knows the Trouble I've Seen*. Some Jewish fellow, not to be outdone, reached for the twins' microphone and began chanting, *"Why is this night different from all other nights?"*

Several people with pale, sickly faces pulled themselves up from the floor by the edge of a table. It was a scene right out of some cheap horror flick as they floundered around in the dim light of the restaurant, stumbling and drooling and making weird guttural sounds. Probo recalled the stories Opie had told him about the twins' effect on people...how excited audiences fell all over themselves like zombies at a hoe-down. "Wow," he exclaimed as one of the pasty-faced figures lunged past him in an attempt to get its hands around the fallen man's throat. "Opie wasn't kidding…they're crazy about us." It wasn't long, however, before Probo realized that something was amiss. Zyg's men were chasing around frantically trying to hold back the crowd, many of whom were crying out in pain and confusion, their pitiful moans more unsettling than anything the twins could muster. The latter, meanwhile, were huddled around the fallen singer, waving their arms about in an effort to fend off his attackers. Probo panicked. He felt he should do something but he didn't know what. Suddenly he remembered an old movie he'd seen in which Wyatt Earp, dressed in black and brandishing a long, sawed-off firearm similar to what the Jews had, broke up a saloon fight by firing his pistol in the air. Probo took a deep breath, raised his trumpet to his lips and with a single blast of air let out the longest, most ear-piercing squeal anyone had ever heard…except for the time Rhoda the Fat Lady sat on Geppetto the midget (not that he hadn't asked her to).

The room fell silent. No one moved a muscle. Then, as if by some evil gust of wind the door to the restaurant flew open and in stepped the disheveled, homeless-looking man Probo had encountered earlier in the alley. He simply stood there with arms spread wide like Moses in the Ten Commandments parting the Red Sea, and proclaimed in a loud, thunderous voice: "Behold…the Day of Judgment is upon thee. Get down on your knees, you sinners, and repent. Repent…and prepare to meet thy Maker."

"What the fuck…?" said Wang, raising himself up on one

elbow. "Who is that bum? Somebody get him out of here...and turn on the lights while you're at it." Once again the man cried out, "Jesus...I have come to offer my humble apologies, and to proclaim that if it is Thy wish to appear before Thy flock in the guise of an elephant...then who am I to question it?"

"An elephant?" said the man with the protective head gear who until now had not been heard from. "Jesus...an elephant? "Jesus was no elephant. Jesus was a Jew."

"Oh, my God," cried Probo as the man with the cataract-covered eyes began feeling his way toward the front of the room. "I've got to get out of here." As the trumpet player struggled to make his way to a nearby exit, the front door of the restaurant once again swung open, this time admitting a couple of curiously-shaped figures whose faces were obscured by the shadows thrown off by the swinging lanterns. Probo nevertheless recognized them as his former bandmates, Shakey and Mumps. Their eyes trawled the room like searchlights, passing over twisted bodies sprawled across the floor or collapsed on tables like the hulks of dead ships. They landed squarely on the elephant as he fumbled with the sliding door leading to the back room of the restaurant. Cornered like a rat in a maze (did someone say *'rat'*...?) he felt his heart sink straight to the bottom of his big, flat feet. "Oh no, I'm ruined...ruined!" he sobbed. The only thought racing through his mind was to get his hands on that big, sawed-off Smith and Wesson of Wang's and blow his brains out. No, he would find it and blow *Wang's* brains out. *Then* he would kill himself. "Wait a minute," he thought, glancing at the clock on the wall. "Shabbas *is* over, isn't it?"

By now the man with the shabby beard and somewhat disoriented demeanor had made his way to the front of the room and was pulling at Probo's collar in an effort to get his attention. "Excuse me, your…er, *Elephantship*," he croaked, spewing poison in the musician's ear. "I know you're kind of busy right now, what with saving souls and raising the dead and all that, but I was wondering…you got any more of that smoke?"

As Zyg's aides rounded up the last of the guests and shuffled them off to cars and buses waiting to take them to their residences, Opie climbed out from behind his drum set and made a beeline for the bedraggled figure in the torn, dirty coat. Running up to him, he looked deep into the stranger's weather-beaten face. The man stared back at the lad with glazed, unseeing eyes. "Daddy, Daddy…is that you?" the drummer shouted, waving his hands frantically in the air. "Daddy, it's me…your son, Opie." At these words the lad's grandmother, huddled in a corner on the far side of the room, glanced up and stared intensely at the older man…then turned pale as a ghost. Amidst the commotion Probo slipped over to a trash receptacle situated a short distance from where Betty sat with her head buried in her hands. Reaching into his suit pocket, he pulled out a crumpled bag which he tossed into the upright container with a sigh of relief. "Never again," he vowed. "I don't care if I go blind. Never again."

"Daddy, Daddy," the freckle-faced lad repeated, screaming into the stranger's face as the latter stared past him, unresponsive to the young man's pleas. "I've been searching for you for over a year. It's me…your son, Opie. Don't you recognize me?"

Finally, the man reached into his coat pocket, pulled out a half pint of vodka, took a long sip from it and said, "What the hell you talking about, kid? I can't see sh...sh...sh...SHIT!"

Betty looked up to find Probo standing a few feet away from her. Shame and regret welled up in her beautiful green eyes. A vulnerable moment for the usually unflappable woman with the small tattoo engraved across her thigh that read '*Ride again...25¢*'. Probo hesitated for an instant. Then he spoke. "Why? Why me? "What did I ever do to you?" he asked, his voice riddled with emotion. Struggling to hold back her tears, Betty managed a reply. "I....I meant well," she stammered, picking herself up and walking slowly toward the grim-faced horn player. "Trying to give Wayne one last chance at the spotlight. I owed it to him, after the way I treated him...so many years ago. You see, Wayne and I had just gotten married...then, a few months later I met Sturgis, Wayne's new trumpet player and one of the stars of the show. I couldn't help myself. Stu was a good deal younger than Wayne and so much more, er...'together' you might say. Besides, I had a young son to raise – Opie's *father*. It was something Wayne just couldn't seem to accept. I've always felt bad about what happened, and for years I've wanted to make it up to him...somehow, some day. Wayne so loves to perform with horns behind him, and you needed a band, so I thought..." Betty put her face into her hands and cried. "I'm so sorry. I didn't think Wayne would still be so crazy after all these years."

"Wayne? Did you say *Wayne*?" Probo sputtered, his mind reeling with confusion. He turned in the direction of the man lying across the stage in the moth-eaten suit with the crushed carnation in the lapel. The grief-stricken Gornish twins kneeling beside him cowered under the intensity of the elephant's glare, then looked away. The shark was nowhere to be seen. "Yes. Wayne Gornisht," Betty continued. That's his real name. He's the twins' father, by another woman, of course - although I've helped raise the girls ever since she died several years ago." Probo's drug-addled mind went down like the Hindenburg in a burst of flame. The *girls...?*

"Yup, that's him all right," said someone with a smirk in his voice. The man adjusted something on his camera. "Wayne Gornisht - small-time band leader from the '30s and '40s who went by the name of Daddy G if I recall. His father was Yehudah 'Bad Boy' Gornisht, the famous trumpet player who performed at Rudolph Valentino's funeral. Came out on the Sabbath just for the chance to honor the silent film star. When he found out the actor's body had been replaced by a wax effigy as a precaution against the hordes of women trying to get at the coffin, he went nuts and jammed the bell of his instrument right into the dummy's balls, or at least where its balls would have been - had someone not already stolen them." The cameraman stepped over to where Wang was struggling to lift himself from the stage. "Smile," he said, pressing his finger to the shutter. "This is your big day." Rearranging his hairpiece, the singer paused, smiled dejectedly and collapsed back into the arms of his sobbing daughters. "If you weren't famous before," said the cameraman, brushing traces of straw from his shoulder, "you will be now...after this fiasco."

"Really?" Wang cried out excitedly as he struggled to his feet. "That's fantastic! Which paper will it be in?" Several other men from the media stood leaning against the wall, laughing hysterically and passing something between them which each in turn pressed tightly to his lips. "Imagine finding all this shit right here in the trash container," said the man with the glassy look in his eyes. "Damn...this is some wicked herb. I can't even feel my hands."

"Is that right?" said the reporter standing next to him with a downward glance. "Well, I hope you can still feel your Johnson...because some old lady is about to cut it off."

Finally someone turned on the lights. The two figures standing in the doorway emerged from the shadows and walked slowly past the overturned chairs and tables, making their way to where the stunned and confused elephant leaned wearily against the wall. "Hello Probo," said the anteater, leaning painfully on his leg and looking greatly fatigued. "We've been searching high and low for you. I'm glad to see you're all right." Mumps tossed aside a banana he'd been working on and joined the conversation. "Yea, our first break was when this guy we know here in Chicago caught sight of Opie's truck with the circus logo on the side and you riding in the back. He asked around a bit and found out about this gathering here tonight, and...well, here we are." Probo stood silent, his head hanging dejectedly, a figure of shame and disgrace. He didn't know what to say. "And we want you to come home with us, back to Pcanutville...if you're willing," Shakey insisted. "We really need you."

"And miss you," the bassoon player piped in, reaching into his pocket for a fresh, green banana. "You do?" replied the elephant, a glimmer of hope twinkling faintly in his eyes. He glanced over to where the homeless man sat quietly with the skinny kid beside him, hugging him close. Looking back at the anteater and his moon-faced companion, Probo asked, "Are you serious? But what about Hornbuckle?"

"Well, you have to realize," explained the anteater, "after you took off the clown was the only one around who could fill in for you on opening day...though he isn't much of a horn player. Nevertheless, we hired him," he added somewhat shamefacedly, "although we told him right from the start it was a temporary arrangement until we could find you and bring you back. We're family, man...we couldn't just let you go. Besides, we fired that crazy bastard a week ago. Some farmer spotted him breaking into his hen house, drunk as hell and wearing nothing but a jockstrap and that big, rubber nose of his. The cops found him lying in a corner with a bird under each arm, singing that old Kinks song over and over to himself, *Where Have All the Good Times Gone?* The chickens were scared shitless. Last I heard they still weren't laying eggs. I've got to tell you, that guy was one weird bird himself. I don't know why the circus master hired him in the first place."

"Weird is right," the orangutan added, wrapping his long arm around his circus buddy. "But you won't have to worry about him any more. I told that miserable geek when he came to pick up his belongings that he'd better never show his face around Peanutville again. I also told him in no uncertain terms that he would never be the horn player that you are. No sirree...not ever. He didn't like that. Got a funny look on his face. Well, good riddance to him."

"Look here, Probo," said the anteater reaching into his shoulder bag and pulling out a long scroll of paper. "We've got something to show you." He held the object up by its corners and let it unravel to the floor. Everyone in the place stood watching...except the guy in the washroom examining his Johnson. Probo thought he was going to cry. Stretched out before him in a bright array of colors was the most beautiful circus poster he had ever seen. And right at the top in big, bold letters it read:

Cecil B. DeMoyel
presents
The **PEANUTVILLE CIRCUS**
Home of the Peanutville Circus Band
With SHAKEY *the Anteater on clarinet*
and Swinger *the Orangutan on bassoon*
- featuring P R O B O *the Elephant on trumpet -*

"We were going to surprise you with it, but you ran off before we had the chance. We'll make sure the printer doesn't screw up again," said Shakey, trying to conceal his embarrassment as he handed the poster to the elephant. Probo accepted it with downcast eyes. "By the way...," the orangutan boasted, pulling yet another piece of fruit from his pocket. "Did you notice I got my old name back again...*Swinger*? After you left I realized I couldn't just sit around feeling sorry for myself...not when my old buddy might be in trouble. I decided it was time I got a grip on myself and started acting like the man I really am. Besides, all those young cows out behind the barn kept asking about you, and I figured you might need some help keeping them company when you got back." Probo laughed and gave his friend a hug. "Of course, you can still call me Mumps," the ape added. "By the way, what was that terrible noise we heard coming up the street? It sounded like a funeral or something. Hey, you're a circus musician, man. You're supposed to be playing happy, cheerful music. Don't you know that?"

"I do now," sobbed Probo as the woman in the Marquis de Sade - Swan Lake outfit stepped over to where everyone was gathered and wrapped her arms meekly around the elephant. Even the sullen twins came down from their dark towers and burst into smiles, while Opie jabbered on happily about how he was going to buy a new truck and let his father drive it on occasion. Wang, too, was beaming with pride for *his* trumpet player. "But what about my floor?" he asked woefully, glancing at the damage strewn about the place. A long shadow fell across his face as he pulled on his wooden shoes and began walking around. *"The fucking pigs,"* he murmured, kicking at a discarded bagel with a pair of yellow dentures clinging to one side.

*****

And so, everything turned out for the best. Opie was at last reunited with his father who, besides being Betty's long lost son, was also Wang's half-brother (it took Probo a month to figure that one out). Opie and his dad returned to Madapahadawanee, where the former circus drummer bought a shiny, new truck and started a long-distance delivery service. Opie did the driving, but every now and then when traffic wasn't too heavy he let the old man slip behind the wheel and take her down the highway while the mule-faced lad hung his skinny ass out the window and mooned at the passing cars.

Wang and Betty reunited after many years and opened a small dance club in Hadapawadamanee, the town where two hundred years before the fierce, half-naked Mawaugatuks and the nattily attired French laid down their arms and opened the first fashion boutique on the North American continent. The happy couple named the place **Bad Boy's** in honor of Wang's late father. Entertainment was provided by the swaggering, dark-haired Gornisht "Brothers", who once again left hard-drinking, cross-dressing Wisconsin lads and lassies ripping it up on the dance floor like zombies at a hoe-down. Betty wore her famous 'chained bear' outfit and welcomed visitors from as far away as Bucyrus who drove all the way in just to see her bow and curtsy. Some of the local farm boys dropped by as well, just to snort and whinny, or whatever it is that farm boys do on Saturday nights. As for the notorious 'Daddy G', he never sang again. He was content just to sit by the fireplace, gazing proudly at news clippings about the 'old folks' riot' - as one Chicago paper called it - and reminiscing about that memorable night back in the Windy City.

Betty's cousin, Zyg, managed to carry his precinct after all that November. Out of 316 registered voters, he carried most of his candidates by a margin of 297 to 63. Out of appreciation the big-wigs downtown named a street after him, while the U.S. Attorney's office named a formal indictment after the champion vote-getter. So the man with the tiny, red balls changed his name to Finkelstein, married the red-headed woman from the diner and moved to Benton Harbor where a few years later he teamed up with his old high school buddy, Paddy McGrafft (but you can call him Pat). Together, they opened an adult book store selling sex toys and sordid novels about back room politics. The most popular item was a small, battery-operated device they called the 'Chicago Machine'. People bought them by the hundreds, just hoping to get screwed. The two men felt right at home.

Back in Peanutville the trio of Shakey, Probo and Mumps became more popular than ever, forging a musical union that folks all over the circus world would be talking about for years. Even Harry the Happy Gelding came around begging to be part of the group. On condition that he find some place other than behind the bandstand to do his business, he was offered a choice spot in the Peanutville Days parade, just steps ahead of the town's mayor and the rest of the dignitaries. Harry didn't let them down. And when the circus crowds in their store-bought monkey suits and OshKosh B'Goshs stood up to join the Fat Lady in a heart-warming rendition of *God Bless America*, they tipped their hats and put their hands together for everyone on stage: the one-legged clarinet player, the fruit-tossing orangutan and especially the trumpet-playing elephant - for it was he that led the assembled mourners in a moment of remembrance for those poor, red- bottomed rhesus monkeys who had thrown themselves from the high wire…just for the shame of it all. Everyone said Probo's long, slow rendition of *Taps* was the most moving lament they had ever heard, but for Probo it was the last sad song he would ever play. Still, he was grateful to his friends up in Wisconsin for having given him the opportunity to learn it.

Time passed and everyone was happy. Rhoda the Fat Lady at last agreed to marry the good Geppetto, provided he get rid of his secret collection of wooden boys. The pretty girls in their skimpy outfits continued to get ants in their pants each time the elephant hit those high C's on his instrument; and needless to say the anteater had no complaints either. But of all the folks in Peanutville, the young trumpet player was the happiest of all… until the day he received an envelope in the mail with no return address. Inside was a single sheet of paper, blank except for something scrawled in at the bottom. Reaching for his glasses, Probo was able to make out the hastily written message, though he didn't quite understand it. Despite the fact that he had long stopped using the medicinal herb that Madam Zuzu had prescribed for him, he could still feel a twinge of paranoia creep into his brain as he examined the letter in front of him. It read:

I'll get you and your monkey friend too

Floppy

Epilogue

The following letter was found among the personal effects of the late Ophelia A. Magnus, known throughout the circus world as *Madam Zuzu*, following her sudden demise due to what authorities have called 'an apparent case of bending time and space one too many times'. The Publisher has included said correspondence in this edition of **Probo's Lament** as part of an agreement reached with attorneys representing the deceased's brother - the clown formerly known as *Hornbuckle* – so as to allow the latter an opportunity to tell his side of the story.

July 16, 1986

Dear Sister:

It has been more than a year since my humiliating expulsion from the circus, which as you know was brought about by a culmination of events - not least of which was that despicable ringmaster's threats to put me back in a clown suit if I didn't show some improvement in my horn playing and become what he called "a productive member of the Peanutville ensemble". Ensemble, my ass...some bozo in a hair-suit and a one-legged clarinet player who likes to eat bugs. Heaven knows I tried, what with the long hours of practice I put in night after night, blowing my heart out on that cheap coronet you bought me in hopes that the light of opportunity might one day shine upon your poor, much maligned brother. Imagine my excitement when that day finally arrived and the elephant ran off from the circus, leaving me to take his place on the Peanutville stage - only later to be rebuked by friends of his who claimed I would never be the "world-class musician" their beloved pachyderm was. Well, you know I did my best, dear sister, despite the fact that the only musical training I had prior to joining this menagerie was riding around on that miserable three-wheeler they gave me, beeping the crap out of the stupid horn mounted on the handlebars. The indignities one has to endure in this business are beyond compare and are made all the more egregious when someone of my stature has to squeeze his entire frame onto the flimsy carriage of some broken-down bike. Added to this was the malicious laughter hurled at me by the crowds while their precious elephant paraded about with his big, shiny horn, drawing rounds of applause for sounding like a stuck pig crying for its mother.

Alas, it's a sad story as you know and one that led me back to the bottle, I am sorry to say. Time was when clowning was a noble profession – back when I traveled with the carnival, greeting visitors and entertaining the youngsters. In those days a clown was larger than life, a hero of sorts...a father figure to many and someone to be admired. A first-class entertainer such as myself brought joy and happiness to others by representing the child that dwells within each of us. If anyone was deserving of ridicule it was those beer-guzzling rabble-rousers who came around the carnival at night thinking to have their way with some of our women. Being the gentleman and gallant that I am, I stepped up at once and volunteered to rid our little community of the vermin, hoping at the same time to win the admiration of the woman I loved. She was an angel, one of the regulars on the circuit...a bit rough around the edges perhaps, but pure as the driven snow. She had this monkey she toted around with her – her grandson, I think – and she liked to stay up late baking cookies and such. I couldn't just stand by and let others sully her reputation with their stories and lies. But even after I showed a bunch of those yahoos what real humiliation was about and sent them packing with their pitchforks in their hands, she had no use for me. Despite my best efforts she continued to spurn my advances. Thus it was that I packed up my clown suit and moved to Hollywood where I could blend in amongst the crowd. That's when the drinking set in. But you know all that, sister, and there's no use going over it.

*And now, here I am looking back on those happy days in Peanutville where, after having reunited with you after so many years, I had pinned my hopes on a glorious future. Instead, I have become an object of derision in the book the elephant reportedly is working on – some piece of trash alleging to tell "the whole story" about why he ran off from the circus and making me out to be some sort of pervert. I hear from the few friends I have left in circus town that the coward doesn't even have the guts to publish this pack of lies under his own name. He's hired some hack writer out of Chicago to do it for him...a guy named **Lubin**. And they say the horse – what's his name, Harry? – has no balls. Really!*

My initial response upon hearing about the so-called book was to mail the elephant an intimidating letter – my intention being to play upon his somewhat paranoid nature as I so effectively did the first time when I had him believing that the anteater was responsible for his name being left off the circus posters. But after mailing the letter I realized there really wasn't much point to it, so I contacted an attorney. Much to my chagrin I was advised that insofar as the events related in the book are factual, any objections I might raise would have little legal standing. Still, my lawyer said he would look into the matter...for a nominal fee, of course.

On a happier note, it pleases me to report that I have been exonerated in another matter, one in which this same extraterrestrial who calls himself an attorney charged me a thousand dollars just to stand up in court and say that I was innocent...which of course I was. It concerned allegations that by operating a small business out of my home I was engaged in activities bordering on what the authorities called "public indecency". I ask you - what's indecent about holding private gatherings of small groups of men that share similar interests? As for the women who were present...I hired them at my own expense as part of the training I offered my clients in order to prepare them for the pitfalls they would encounter while running for public office here in Chicago. Keep in mind, dear sister, these are not the sort of individuals for whom sex is just another one of life's little pleasures, like smoking a fine cigar. These are men of character and high ideals, born to hold important positions in government and who are little versed in the ways of the world. That's why, when they do get caught up in some highly-publicized scandal, it's such a messy affair...kind of like those trick cigars I pass out that explode in your face.

As I've said, the idea behind this little school of mine was to help prospective candidates prepare themselves for the challenges they would face while seeking elected office here in Chicago. After all, who knows more about the cruelty and fickleness of the crowd than I? Even the judge agreed that there was nothing improper in this little business enterprise of mine. Still, I imagine it helped when my attorney placed into evidence several photographs of the judge's brother-in-law, a candidate for City Treasurer, posing with a group of scantily-clad women and wearing nothing but a pair of jockey shorts and a big, rubber nose. Like I've always said, you can never have too much insurance.

Anyway, I am getting by, having given up the clown school and taken to driving a cab. Chicago is a pretty decent town. They appreciate strangers here and are generous with their tips. In fact, I make a bit more than I did working for the circus...not that old man DeMoyel didn't offer me a decent wage when he hired me; but that rotten nephew of his who serves as ringmaster and who hates my guts made sure I never collected all I was entitled to.

I hear through the grapevine that the elephant was here in the Windy City about a year ago, but left shortly before I arrived. Apparently the "world-class" trumpet player didn't make much of an impression. No one remembers him – except this little old lady who rode in my cab one day. We were driving past some boarded-up restaurant, when suddenly she blurted out, "My God, that's where my husband had his heart attack and died right before my eyes...in the men's room." She went on to say that it was all hush-hush due to political connections the restaurant owner had through some friend of his. Apparently, everyone assumed that the fellow who owned the place was responsible for what happened; but according to the old lady the elephant was somehow involved, wrapping "that long, ugly thing of his" - as she called it - around her waist and asking if she would like to step into the back room and share a bag of peanuts. There was this stupid-looking kid with him, egging him on...calling him "Casanova" and urging him to "go for it". The woman's husband overheard the conversation and was so distraught that he rushed to the men's room to throw some cold water on his face. Once he got there he was accosted by some guy acting all crazy and whatnot who ran up to him, screaming, "My God...look at my Johnson!" At least that's what the woman's husband told her just before he died. I must confess, sister, that I took more than a little satisfaction in hearing the old lady's story – not because of her poor husband, may he rest in peace, but in knowing that the former kazoo player that everyone so adores has to live with his deep, dark secret. Well, maybe the wonder-boy actually believes he's the innocent darling people have been telling him he is all his life. After all, we all have our illusions, and certainly I have mine...but at least they are my own.

Forgive me for sharing the following "indelicacy" with you, but I think it important to show that I am not alone in the animus I bear toward the elephant – though I am trying to get over it, given that I too am to blame for much of what has transpired and for involving you in this sordid affair. Just before I dropped the old woman off at the sad-looking retirement home where she lived, she turned to me and said with a drawn and bitter face, "As far as I'm concerned, the guy in the men's room and that hideous beast should both rot in hell." Without thinking, I immediately shot back, "Oh, is he dead?" – to which she responded, "Well, if not then his Johnson should rot in hell."

But enough said, dear sister. You know my situation and there's no point in troubling you with these dark offerings of the soul. My best to you, and all my love...and say hello to the old man who takes care of the animals. We had some good times together, the three of us. And remember to watch your back. There are some pretty unsavory characters in that two-bit circus where you work. God forgive me for having been one of them.

Your loving brother,
Sachel

Postscript

Wayne Gornisht, a.k.a. 'Daddy G', died in his sleep on March 22, 2001 at the age of 92. He was buried in Wangtree, Oklahoma with his news clippings in his pocket and his gun in his pants. The Gornisht twins performed at his funeral.

GLOSSARY

Cecil B. DeMoyel - founder and owner of the Peanutville Circus, which first raised its tents in 1927

gornisht - Yiddish word meaning 'nothing'

meshugener - a crazy person (Yiddish)

sable - a greasy form of smoked cod

schmaltz herring - a fatty form of herring, preserved in brine

Shabbas - Saturday, the Jewish Sabbath

the 'Spice' - drug mentioned in Frank Herbert's sci-fi novel *DUNE,* which enables its user to bend time and space

tanna leaves - as mentioned in the old 'Mummy' flicks of the '30s and '40s. Used to keep the creature alive

Wyatt Earp - famous lawman of the Old West, known for his well-tailored suits and the 12-inch 'Buntline Special' he sported

Yontif - Yiddish for holiday, as in the expression *'Good Yontif',* normally said around Rosh Hashanah, the Jewish New Year

Zadie - affectionate term for grandfather (Yiddish)

Gene Lubin is a Chicago writer and the publisher of New American Storybook. He is currently working on a compilation of original writings by the clown known as Hornbuckle, with a scheduled release date of 2010.

Howard Berkman, who did the illustrations for **Probo's Lament,** is a well-known singer/songwriter and guitarist originally from Chicago. He currently resides in Colorado.